My Little Pony™

Pony Tales

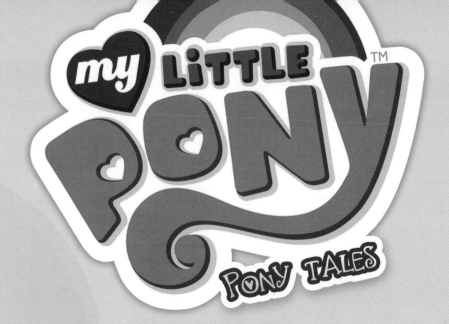

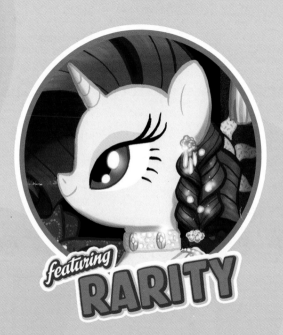

featuring
RARITY

STORY BY Katie Cook

ART BY Andy Price

COLORS BY Heather Breckel

LETTERS BY Neil Uyetake

ABDO Spotlight

IDW

ABDOPUBLISHING.COM

Reinforced library bound edition published in 2015 by Spotlight,
a division of ABDO, PO Box 398166, Minneapolis, Minnesota 55439.
Spotlight produces high-quality reinforced library bound editions for
schools and libraries. Published by agreement with IDW.

Printed in the United States of America, North Mankato, Minnesota.
112014
012015

 THIS BOOK CONTAINS
RECYCLED MATERIALS

LIBRARY OF CONGRESS CATALOGING-IN-PUBLICATION DATA

Cook, Katie, 1981-
  Rarity / writer, Katie Cook ; artist, Andy Price. -- Reinforced library bound
edition.
     pages cm. -- (My little pony. Pony tales)
  Summary: "Rarity goes on a spa vacation that doesn't turn out like she
expected"-- Provided by publisher.
  ISBN 978-1-61479-335-9
1. Graphic novels. I. Price, Andy, illustrator. II. Title.
  PZ7.7.C666Rar 2015
  741.5'973--dc23

                    2014036758

Spotlight

A Division of ABDO
abdopublishing.com

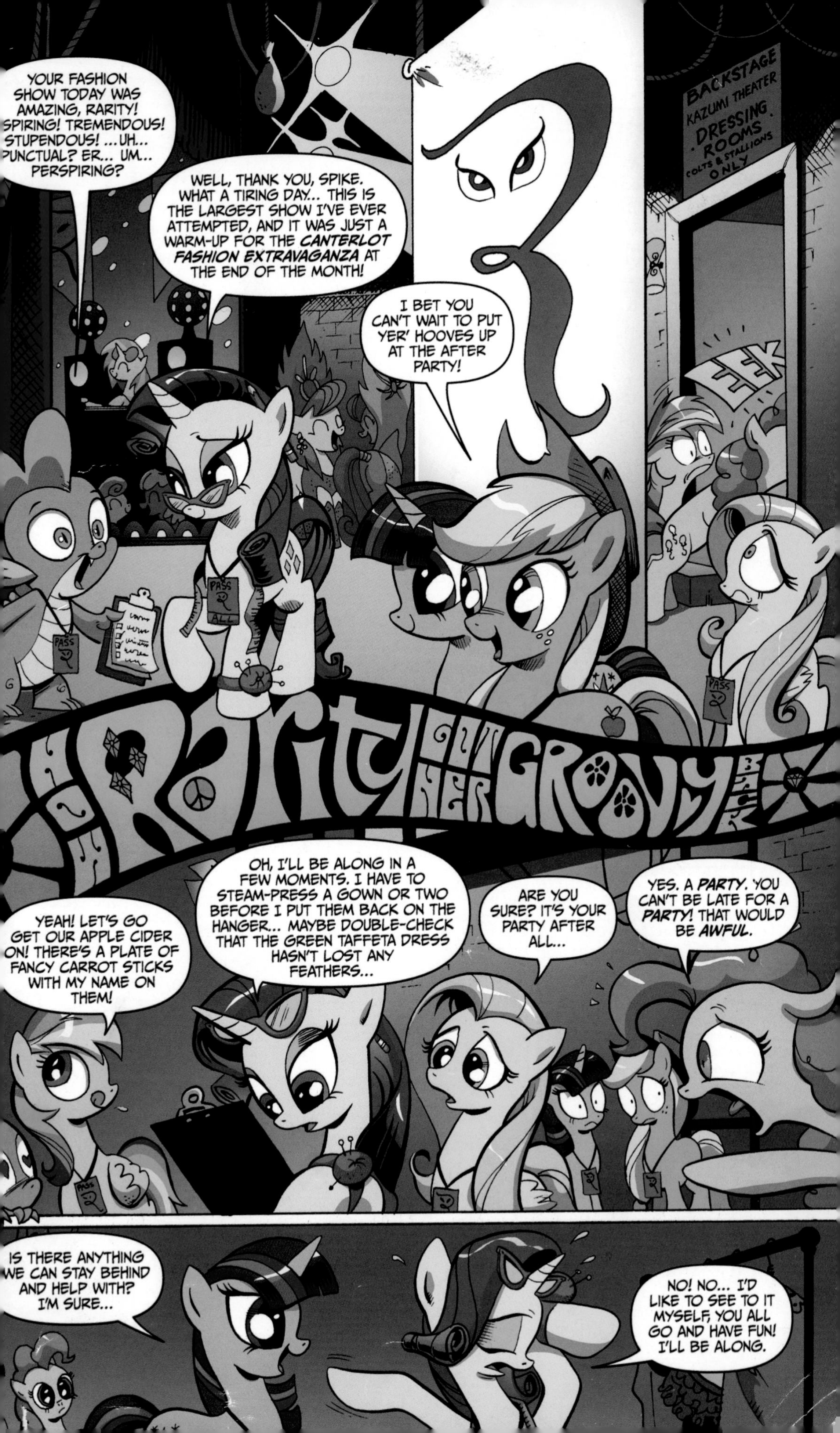
YOUR FASHION SHOW TODAY WAS AMAZING, RARITY! SPIRING! TREMENDOUS! STUPENDOUS! ...UH... PUNCTUAL? ER... UM... PERSPIRING?
WELL, THANK YOU, SPIKE. WHAT A TIRING DAY... THIS IS THE LARGEST SHOW I'VE EVER ATTEMPTED, AND IT WAS JUST A WARM-UP FOR THE *CANTERLOT FASHION EXTRAVAGANZA* AT THE END OF THE MONTH!
BACKSTAGE KAZUMI THEATER DRESSING ROOMS COLTS & STALLIONS ONLY
I BET YOU CAN'T WAIT TO PUT YER' HOOVES UP AT THE AFTER PARTY!
EEK
PASS
PASS ALL
RARITY
HER GROOVY
YEAH! LET'S GO GET OUR APPLE CIDER ON! THERE'S A PLATE OF FANCY CARROT STICKS WITH MY NAME ON THEM!
OH, I'LL BE ALONG IN A FEW MOMENTS. I HAVE TO STEAM-PRESS A GOWN OR TWO BEFORE I PUT THEM BACK ON THE HANGER... MAYBE DOUBLE-CHECK THAT THE GREEN TAFFETA DRESS HASN'T LOST ANY FEATHERS...
ARE YOU SURE? IT'S YOUR PARTY AFTER ALL...
YES. A *PARTY*. YOU CAN'T BE LATE FOR A *PARTY*! THAT WOULD BE *AWFUL*.
IS THERE ANYTHING WE CAN STAY BEHIND AND HELP WITH? I'M SURE...
NO! NO... I'D LIKE TO SEE TO IT MYSELF, YOU ALL GO AND HAVE FUN! I'LL BE ALONG.

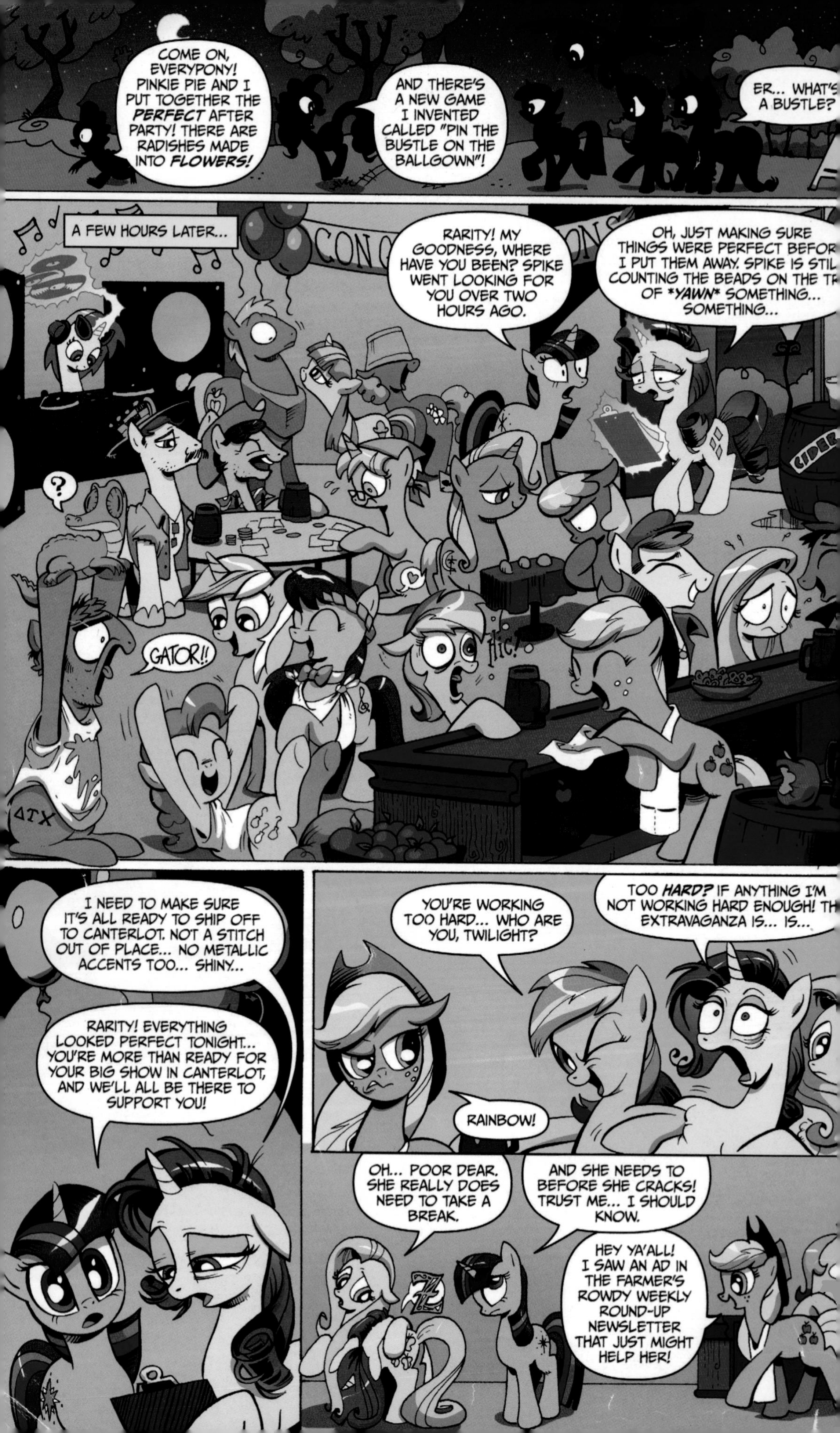
COME ON, EVERYPONY! PINKIE PIE AND I PUT TOGETHER THE *PERFECT* AFTER PARTY! THERE ARE RADISHES MADE INTO *FLOWERS!*
AND THERE'S A NEW GAME I INVENTED CALLED "PIN THE BUSTLE ON THE BALLGOWN"!
ER... WHAT'S A BUSTLE?
A FEW HOURS LATER...
CON
RARITY! MY GOODNESS, WHERE HAVE YOU BEEN? SPIKE WENT LOOKING FOR YOU OVER TWO HOURS AGO.
OH, JUST MAKING SURE THINGS WERE PERFECT BEFOR I PUT THEM AWAY. SPIKE IS STIL COUNTING THE BEADS ON THE TR OF *YAWN* SOMETHING... SOMETHING...
CIDER
GATOR!!
HIC!
ΔTX
I NEED TO MAKE SURE IT'S ALL READY TO SHIP OFF TO CANTERLOT. NOT A STITCH OUT OF PLACE... NO METALLIC ACCENTS TOO... SHINY...
RARITY! EVERYTHING LOOKED PERFECT TONIGHT... YOU'RE MORE THAN READY FOR YOUR BIG SHOW IN CANTERLOT, AND WE'LL ALL BE THERE TO SUPPORT YOU!
YOU'RE WORKING TOO HARD... WHO ARE YOU, TWILIGHT?
TOO *HARD?* IF ANYTHING I'M NOT WORKING HARD ENOUGH! TH EXTRAVAGANZA IS... IS...
RAINBOW!
OH... POOR DEAR. SHE REALLY DOES NEED TO TAKE A BREAK.
AND SHE NEEDS TO BEFORE SHE CRACKS! TRUST ME... I SHOULD KNOW.
HEY YA'ALL! I SAW AN AD IN THE FARMER'S ROWDY WEEKLY ROUND-UP NEWSLETTER THAT JUST MIGHT HELP HER!

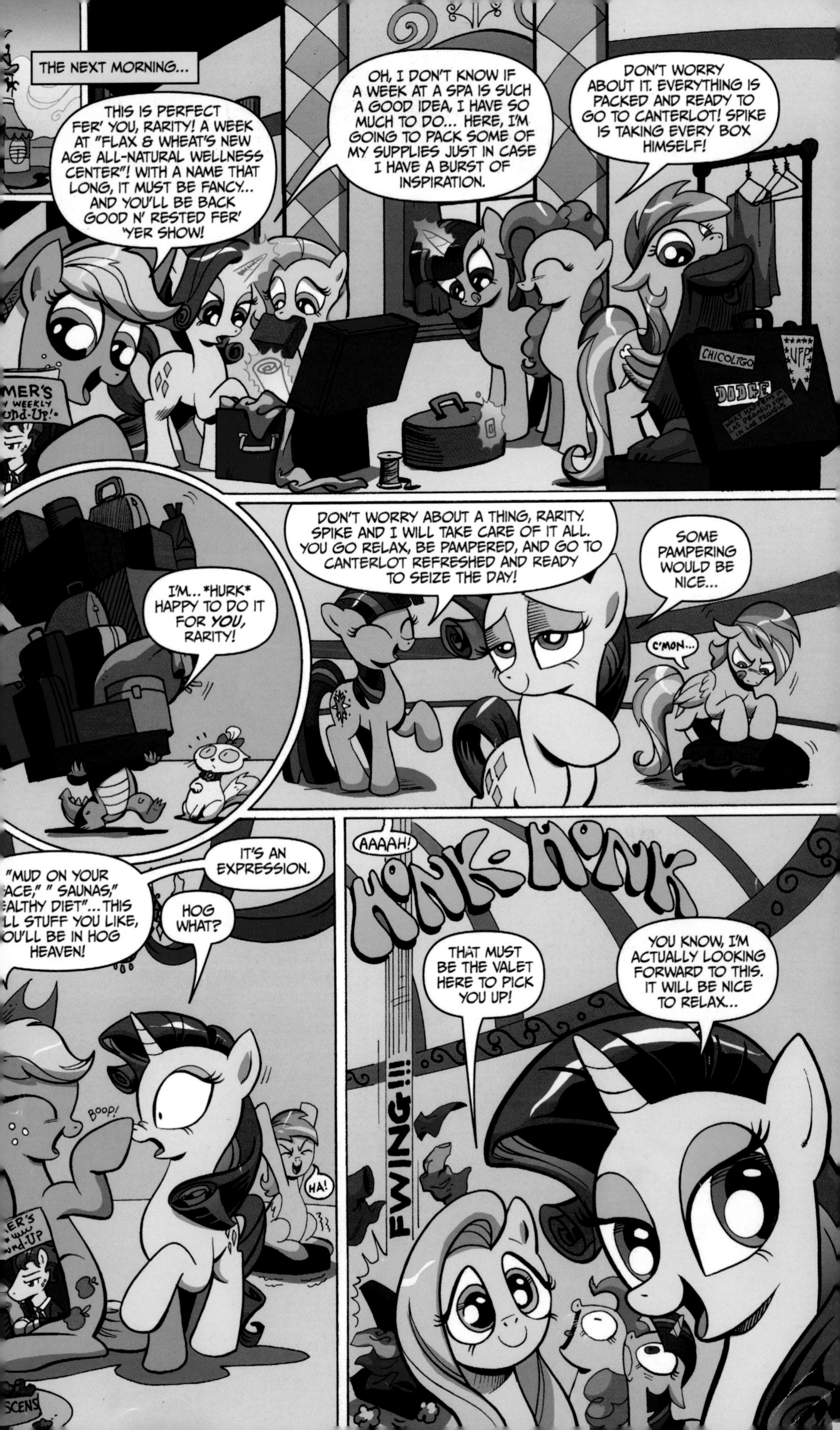
THE NEXT MORNING...
THIS IS PERFECT FER' YOU, RARITY! A WEEK AT "FLAX & WHEAT'S NEW AGE ALL-NATURAL WELLNESS CENTER"! WITH A NAME THAT LONG, IT MUST BE FANCY... AND YOU'LL BE BACK GOOD N' RESTED FER' 'YER SHOW!
OH, I DON'T KNOW IF A WEEK AT A SPA IS SUCH A GOOD IDEA, I HAVE SO MUCH TO DO... HERE, I'M GOING TO PACK SOME OF MY SUPPLIES JUST IN CASE I HAVE A BURST OF INSPIRATION.
DON'T WORRY ABOUT IT. EVERYTHING IS PACKED AND READY TO GO TO CANTERLOT! SPIKE IS TAKING EVERY BOX HIMSELF!
CHICOLTGO
DODGE
I'M... *HURK* HAPPY TO DO IT FOR *YOU*, RARITY!
DON'T WORRY ABOUT A THING, RARITY. SPIKE AND I WILL TAKE CARE OF IT ALL. YOU GO RELAX, BE PAMPERED, AND GO TO CANTERLOT REFRESHED AND READY TO SEIZE THE DAY!
SOME PAMPERING WOULD BE NICE...
C'MON...
"MUD ON YOUR ACE," " SAUNAS," EALTHY DIET"... THIS LL STUFF YOU LIKE, OU'LL BE IN HOG HEAVEN!
IT'S AN EXPRESSION.
HOG WHAT?
BOOP!
HA!
AAAAH!
HONK-HONK
FWING!!!
THAT MUST BE THE VALET HERE TO PICK YOU UP!
YOU KNOW, I'M ACTUALLY LOOKING FORWARD TO THIS. IT WILL BE NICE TO RELAX...

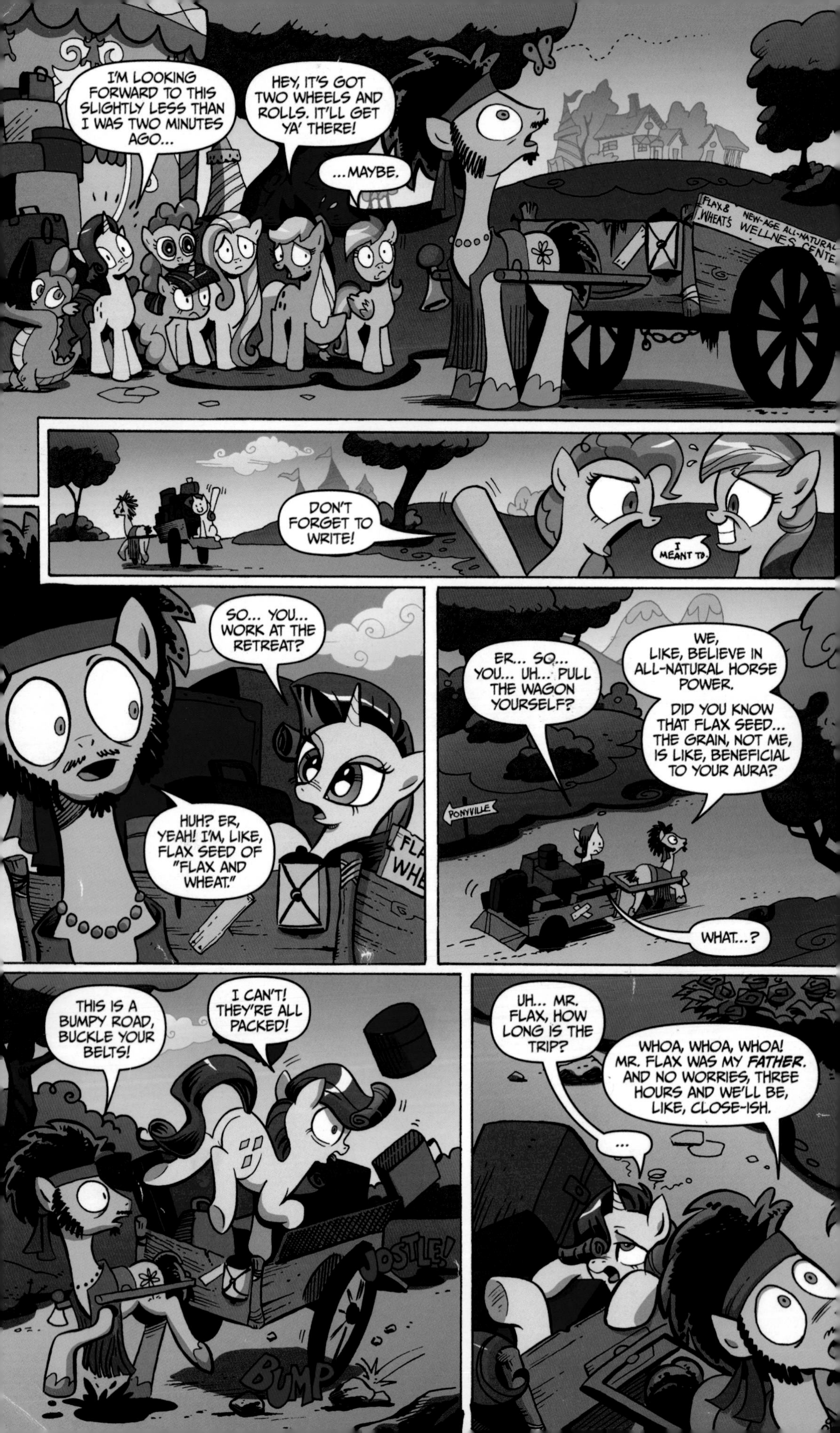
I'M LOOKING FORWARD TO THIS SLIGHTLY LESS THAN I WAS TWO MINUTES AGO...
HEY, IT'S GOT TWO WHEELS AND ROLLS. IT'LL GET YA' THERE!
...MAYBE.
FLAX & WHEAT'S NEW-AGE ALL-NATURAL WELLNES CENTE
DON'T FORGET TO WRITE!
I MEANT TO.
SO... YOU... WORK AT THE RETREAT?
HUH? ER, YEAH! I'M, LIKE, FLAX SEED OF "FLAX AND WHEAT."
ER... SO... YOU... UH... PULL THE WAGON YOURSELF?
WE, LIKE, BELIEVE IN ALL-NATURAL HORSE POWER.
DID YOU KNOW THAT FLAX SEED... THE GRAIN, NOT ME, IS LIKE, BENEFICIAL TO YOUR AURA?
PONYVILLE
WHAT...?
THIS IS A BUMPY ROAD, BUCKLE YOUR BELTS!
I CAN'T! THEY'RE ALL PACKED!
JOSTLE!
BUMP
UH... MR. FLAX, HOW LONG IS THE TRIP?
WHOA, WHOA, WHOA! MR. FLAX WAS MY *FATHER*. AND NO WORRIES, THREE HOURS AND WE'LL BE, LIKE, CLOSE-ISH.
...

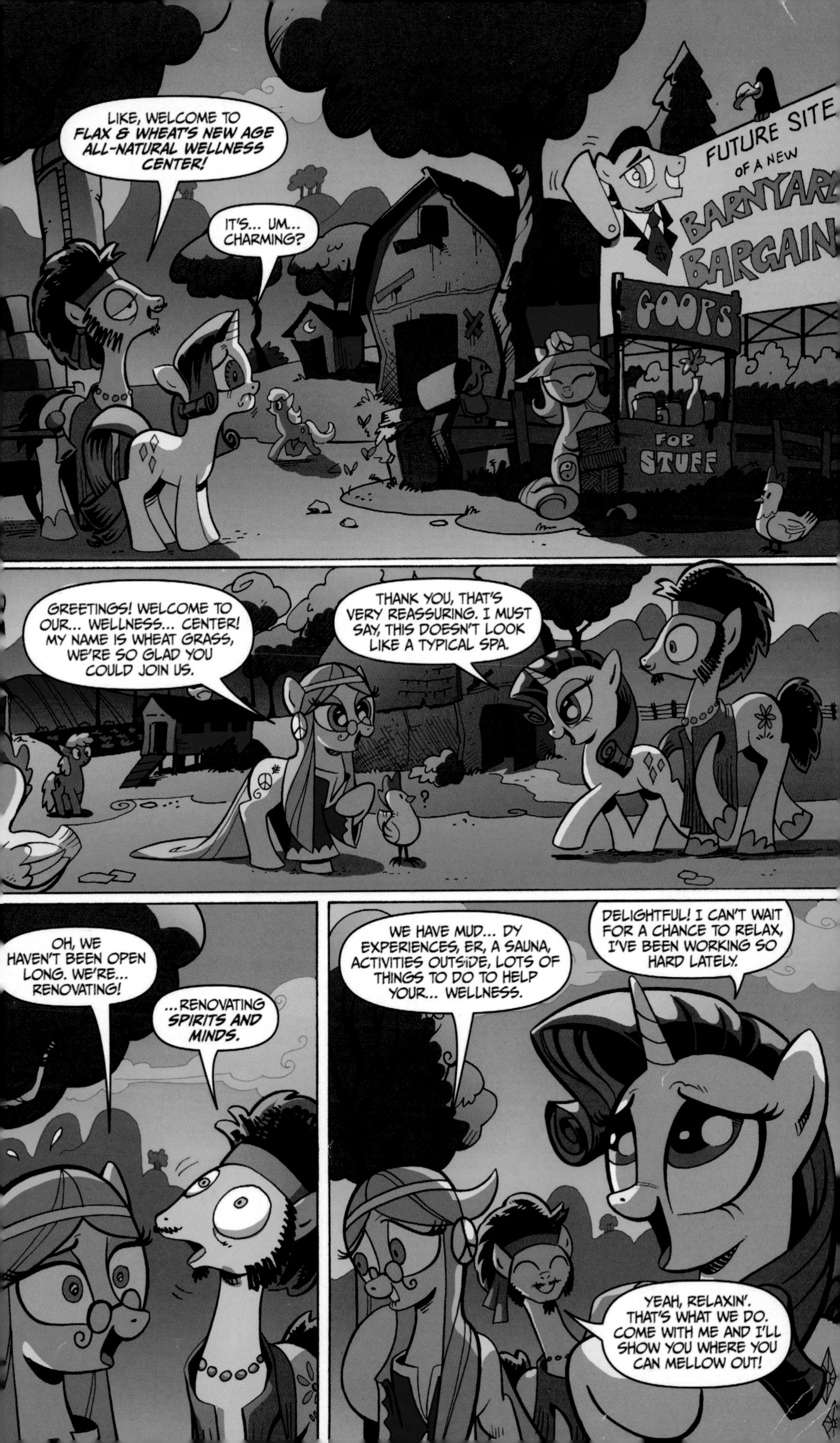
LIKE, WELCOME TO FLAX & WHEAT'S NEW AGE ALL-NATURAL WELLNESS CENTER!
IT'S... UM... CHARMING?
FUTURE SITE OF A NEW BARNYARD BARGAIN
GOOPS
FOR STUFF
GREETINGS! WELCOME TO OUR... WELLNESS... CENTER! MY NAME IS WHEAT GRASS, WE'RE SO GLAD YOU COULD JOIN US.
THANK YOU, THAT'S VERY REASSURING. I MUST SAY, THIS DOESN'T LOOK LIKE A TYPICAL SPA.
OH, WE HAVEN'T BEEN OPEN LONG. WE'RE... RENOVATING!
...RENOVATING SPIRITS AND MINDS.
WE HAVE MUD... DY EXPERIENCES, ER, A SAUNA, ACTIVITIES OUTSIDE, LOTS OF THINGS TO DO TO HELP YOUR... WELLNESS.
DELIGHTFUL! I CAN'T WAIT FOR A CHANCE TO RELAX, I'VE BEEN WORKING SO HARD LATELY.
YEAH, RELAXIN'. THAT'S WHAT WE DO. COME WITH ME AND I'LL SHOW YOU WHERE YOU CAN MELLOW OUT!

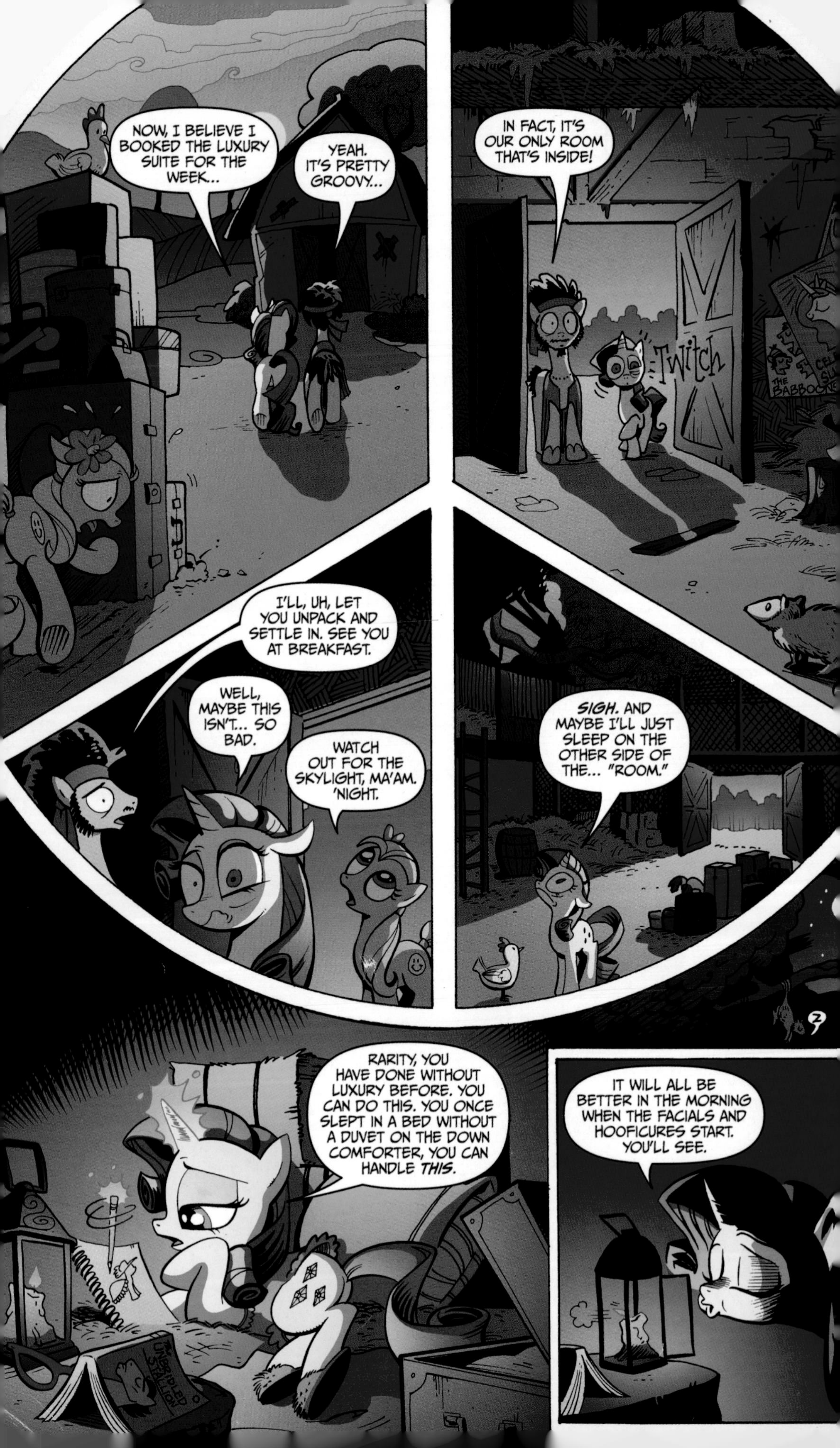
NOW, I BELIEVE I BOOKED THE LUXURY SUITE FOR THE WEEK...
YEAH. IT'S PRETTY GROOVY...
IN FACT, IT'S OUR ONLY ROOM THAT'S INSIDE!
TWITCH
THE BABBOONS
I'LL, UH, LET YOU UNPACK AND SETTLE IN. SEE YOU AT BREAKFAST.
WELL, MAYBE THIS ISN'T... SO BAD.
WATCH OUT FOR THE SKYLIGHT, MA'AM. 'NIGHT.
SIGH. AND MAYBE I'LL JUST SLEEP ON THE OTHER SIDE OF THE... "ROOM."
RARITY, YOU HAVE DONE WITHOUT LUXURY BEFORE. YOU CAN DO THIS. YOU ONCE SLEPT IN A BED WITHOUT A DUVET ON THE DOWN COMFORTER, YOU CAN HANDLE *THIS*.
THE UNBRIDLED STALLION
IT WILL ALL BE BETTER IN THE MORNING WHEN THE FACIALS AND HOOFICURES START. YOU'LL SEE.

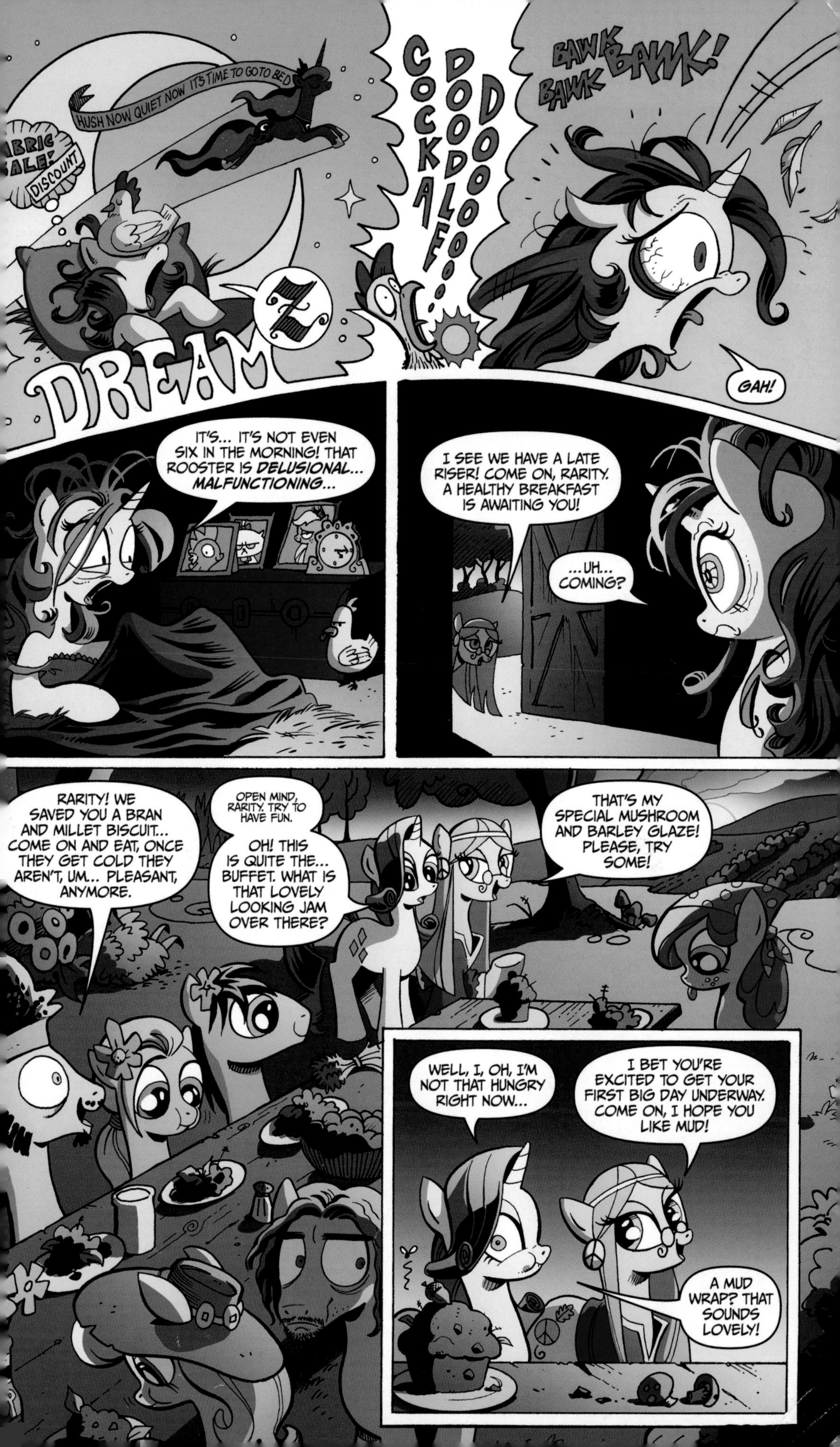
HUSH NOW QUIET NOW IT'S TIME TO GO TO BED
DISCOUNT
DREAM
Z
COCKADOODLEDOO
DOODLEDOOOO...
BAWK BAWK BAWK!
GAH!
IT'S... IT'S NOT EVEN SIX IN THE MORNING! THAT ROOSTER IS DELUSIONAL... MALFUNCTIONING...
I SEE WE HAVE A LATE RISER! COME ON, RARITY. A HEALTHY BREAKFAST IS AWAITING YOU!
...UH... COMING?
RARITY! WE SAVED YOU A BRAN AND MILLET BISCUIT... COME ON AND EAT, ONCE THEY GET COLD THEY AREN'T, UM... PLEASANT, ANYMORE.
OPEN MIND, RARITY. TRY TO HAVE FUN.
OH! THIS IS QUITE THE... BUFFET. WHAT IS THAT LOVELY LOOKING JAM OVER THERE?
THAT'S MY SPECIAL MUSHROOM AND BARLEY GLAZE! PLEASE, TRY SOME!
WELL, I, OH, I'M NOT THAT HUNGRY RIGHT NOW...
I BET YOU'RE EXCITED TO GET YOUR FIRST BIG DAY UNDERWAY. COME ON, I HOPE YOU LIKE MUD!
A MUD WRAP? THAT SOUNDS LOVELY!

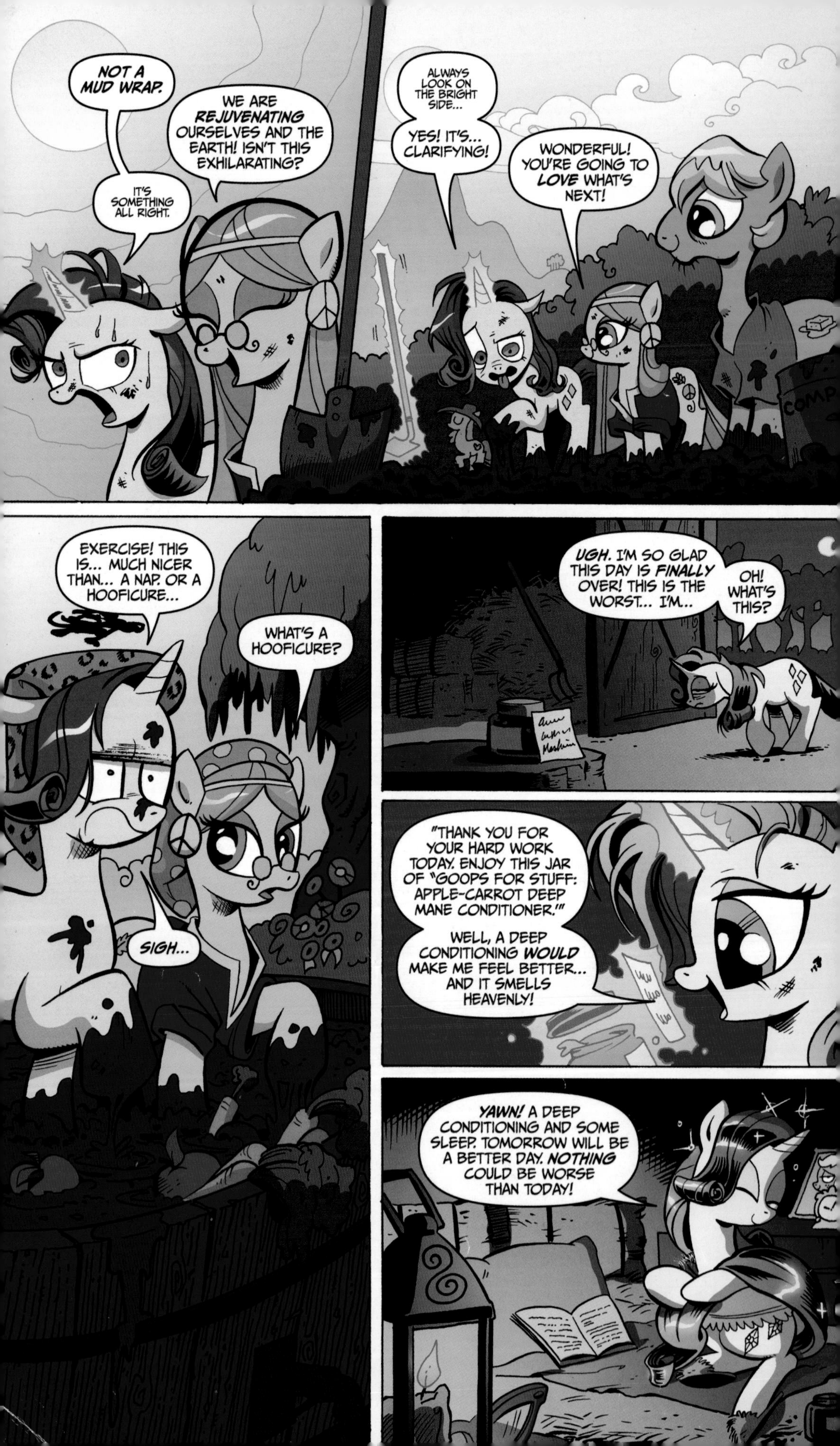
NOT A MUD WRAP.
WE ARE REJUVENATING OURSELVES AND THE EARTH! ISN'T THIS EXHILARATING?
IT'S SOMETHING ALL RIGHT.
ALWAYS LOOK ON THE BRIGHT SIDE...
YES! IT'S... CLARIFYING!
WONDERFUL! YOU'RE GOING TO LOVE WHAT'S NEXT!
COMP
EXERCISE! THIS IS... MUCH NICER THAN... A NAP. OR A HOOFICURE...
WHAT'S A HOOFICURE?
SIGH...
UGH. I'M SO GLAD THIS DAY IS FINALLY OVER! THIS IS THE WORST... I'M...
OH! WHAT'S THIS?
"THANK YOU FOR YOUR HARD WORK TODAY. ENJOY THIS JAR OF "GOOPS FOR STUFF: APPLE-CARROT DEEP MANE CONDITIONER.""
WELL, A DEEP CONDITIONING WOULD MAKE ME FEEL BETTER... AND IT SMELLS HEAVENLY!
YAWN! A DEEP CONDITIONING AND SOME SLEEP. TOMORROW WILL BE A BETTER DAY. NOTHING COULD BE WORSE THAN TODAY!

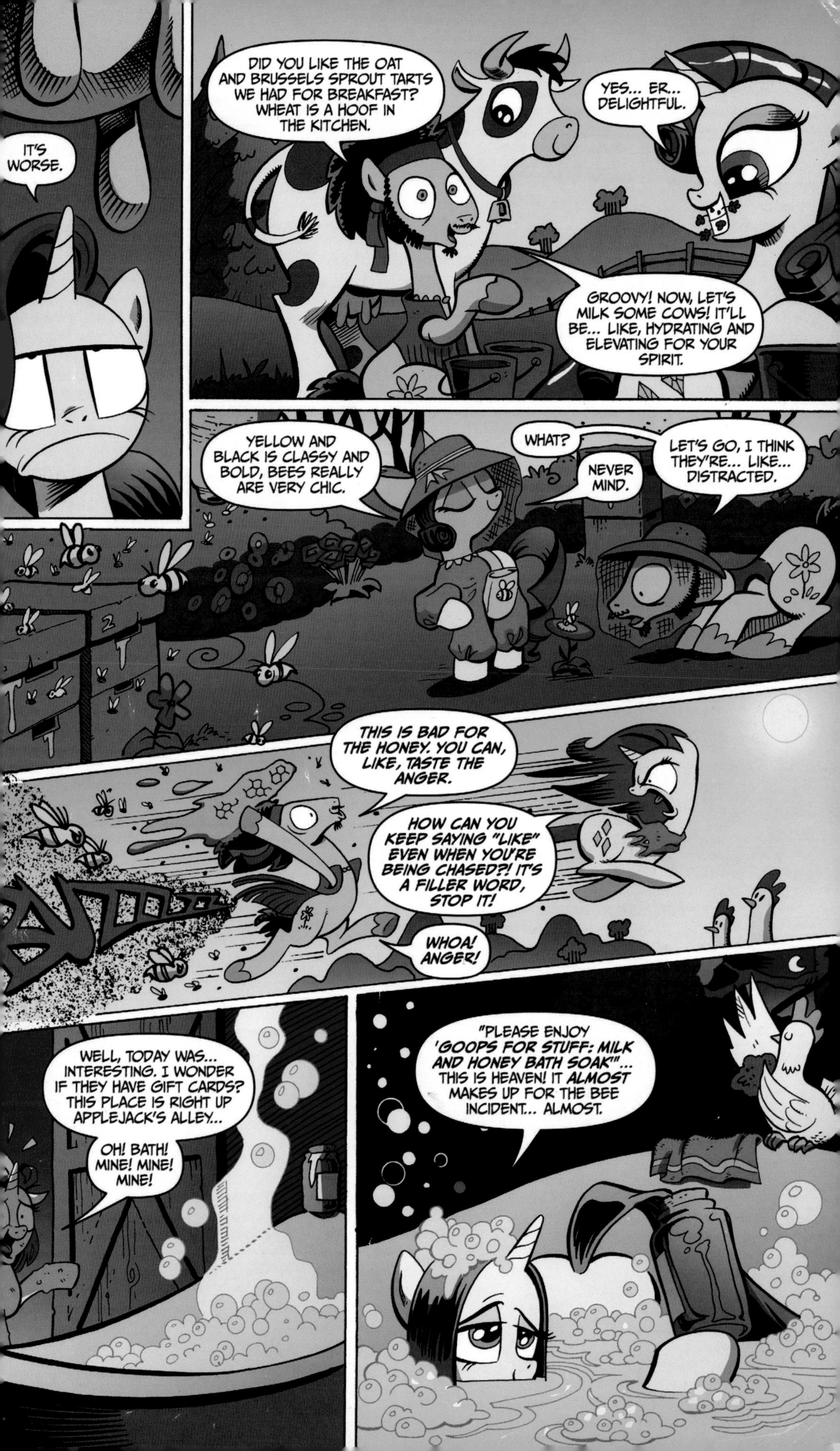
IT'S WORSE.
DID YOU LIKE THE OAT AND BRUSSELS SPROUT TARTS WE HAD FOR BREAKFAST? WHEAT IS A HOOF IN THE KITCHEN.
YES... ER... DELIGHTFUL.
GROOVY! NOW, LET'S MILK SOME COWS! IT'LL BE... LIKE, HYDRATING AND ELEVATING FOR YOUR SPIRIT.
YELLOW AND BLACK IS CLASSY AND BOLD, BEES REALLY ARE VERY CHIC.
WHAT?
NEVER MIND.
LET'S GO, I THINK THEY'RE... LIKE... DISTRACTED.
THIS IS BAD FOR THE HONEY. YOU CAN, LIKE, TASTE THE ANGER.
HOW CAN YOU KEEP SAYING "LIKE" EVEN WHEN YOU'RE BEING CHASED?! IT'S A FILLER WORD, STOP IT!
WHOA! ANGER!
WELL, TODAY WAS... INTERESTING. I WONDER IF THEY HAVE GIFT CARDS? THIS PLACE IS RIGHT UP APPLEJACK'S ALLEY...
OH! BATH! MINE! MINE! MINE!
"PLEASE ENJOY 'GOOPS FOR STUFF: MILK AND HONEY BATH SOAK'"... THIS IS HEAVEN! IT ALMOST MAKES UP FOR THE BEE INCIDENT... ALMOST.

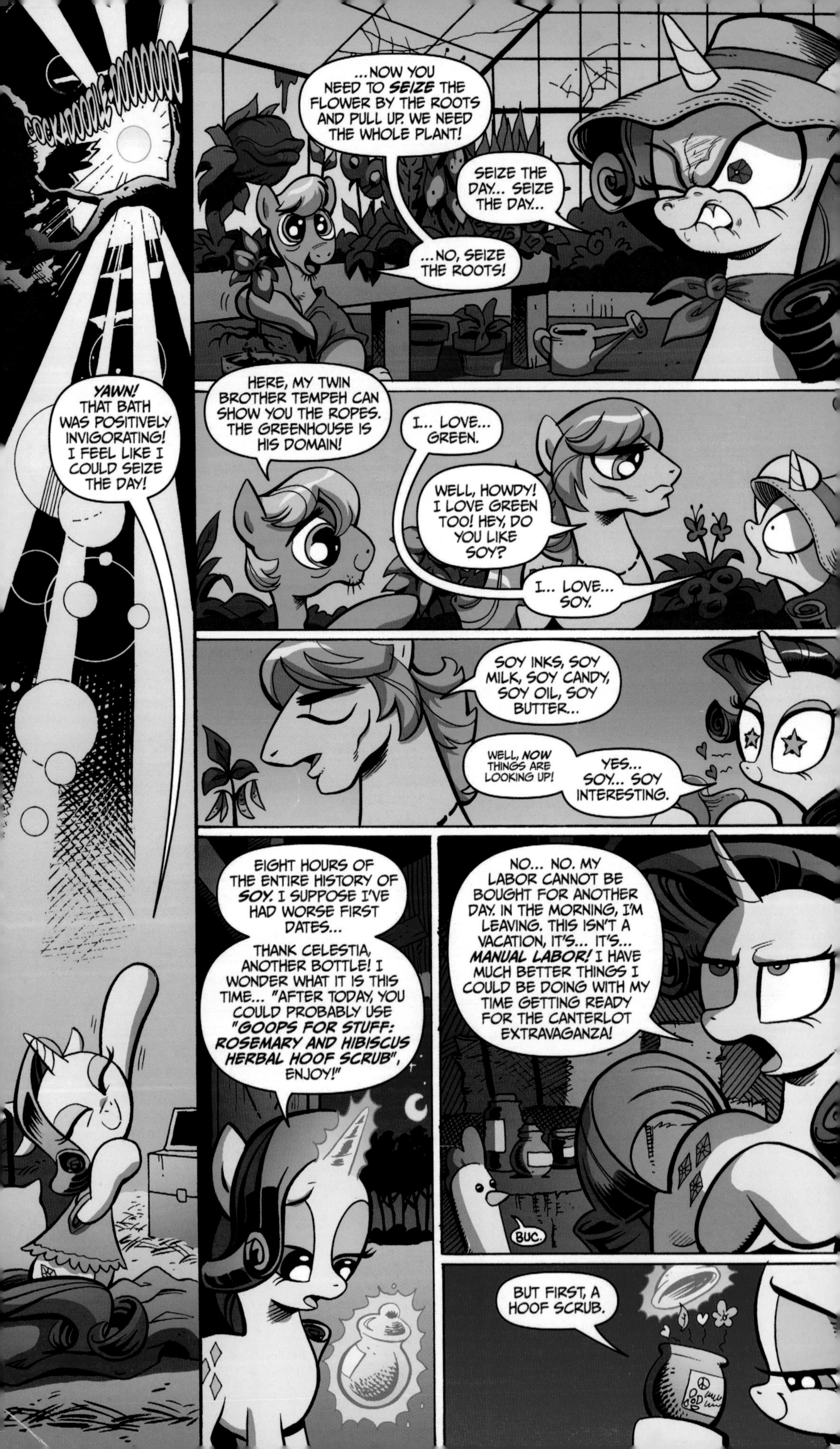
COCKADOODLE-DOOOOOOO
...NOW YOU NEED TO **SEIZE** THE FLOWER BY THE ROOTS AND PULL UP. WE NEED THE WHOLE PLANT!
SEIZE THE DAY... SEIZE THE DAY...
...NO, SEIZE THE ROOTS!
YAWN! THAT BATH WAS POSITIVELY INVIGORATING! I FEEL LIKE I COULD SEIZE THE DAY!
HERE, MY TWIN BROTHER TEMPEH CAN SHOW YOU THE ROPES. THE GREENHOUSE IS HIS DOMAIN!
I... LOVE... GREEN.
WELL, HOWDY! I LOVE GREEN TOO! HEY, DO YOU LIKE SOY?
I... LOVE... SOY.
SOY INKS, SOY MILK, SOY CANDY, SOY OIL, SOY BUTTER...
WELL, ***NOW*** THINGS ARE LOOKING UP!
YES... SOY... SOY INTERESTING.
EIGHT HOURS OF THE ENTIRE HISTORY OF ***SOY.*** I SUPPOSE I'VE HAD WORSE FIRST DATES...
THANK CELESTIA, ANOTHER BOTTLE! I WONDER WHAT IT IS THIS TIME... "AFTER TODAY, YOU COULD PROBABLY USE ***"GOOPS FOR STUFF: ROSEMARY AND HIBISCUS HERBAL HOOF SCRUB"***, ENJOY!"
NO... NO. MY LABOR CANNOT BE BOUGHT FOR ANOTHER DAY. IN THE MORNING, I'M LEAVING. THIS ISN'T A VACATION, IT'S... IT'S... ***MANUAL LABOR!*** I HAVE MUCH BETTER THINGS I COULD BE DOING WITH MY TIME GETTING READY FOR THE CANTERLOT EXTRAVAGANZA!
BUC.
BUT FIRST, A HOOF SCRUB.

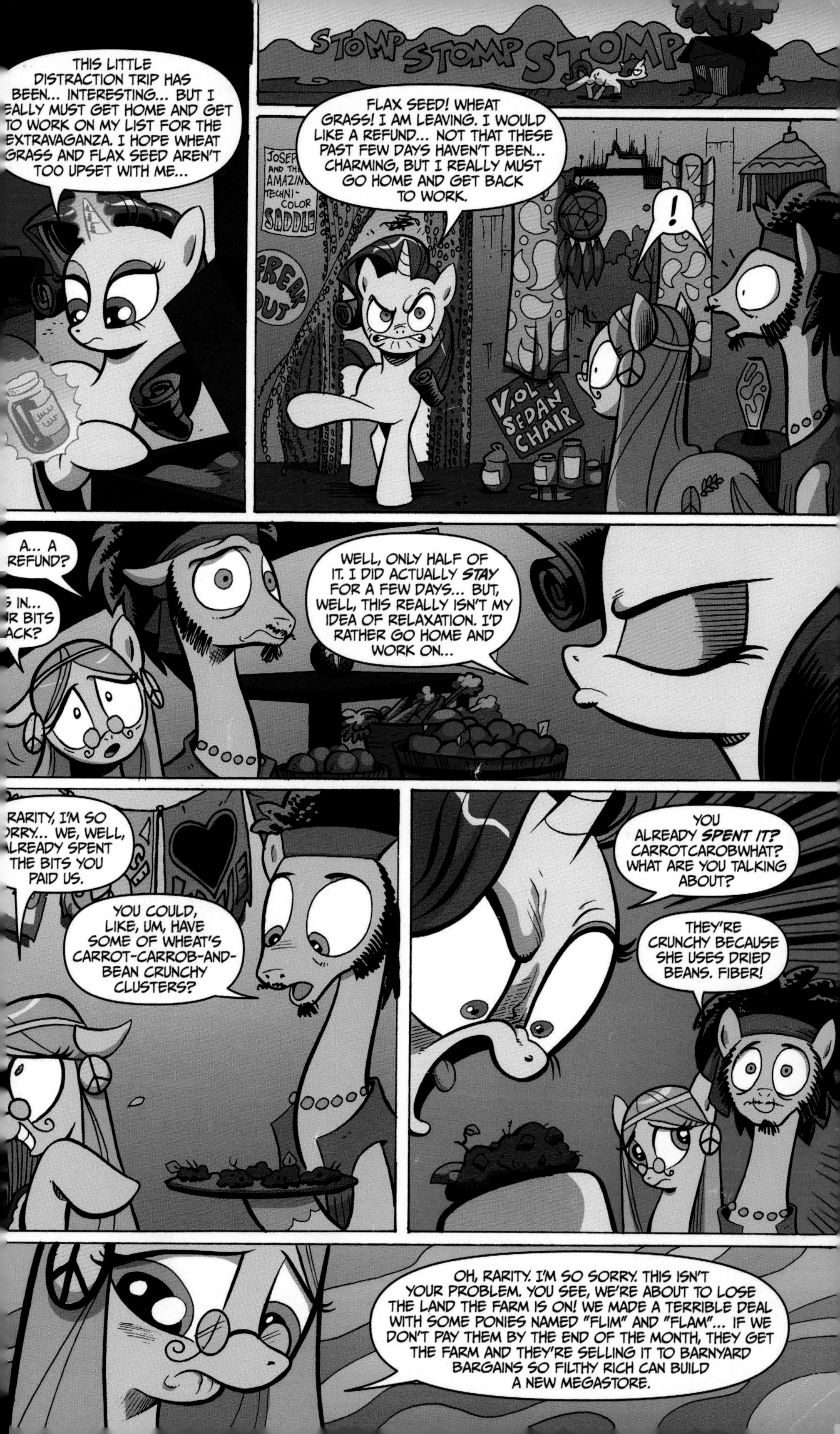
THIS LITTLE DISTRACTION TRIP HAS BEEN... INTERESTING... BUT I EALLY MUST GET HOME AND GET TO WORK ON MY LIST FOR THE EXTRAVAGANZA. I HOPE WHEAT GRASS AND FLAX SEED AREN'T TOO UPSET WITH ME...
STOMP STOMP STOMP
FLAX SEED! WHEAT GRASS! I AM LEAVING. I WOULD LIKE A REFUND... NOT THAT THESE PAST FEW DAYS HAVEN'T BEEN... CHARMING, BUT I REALLY MUST GO HOME AND GET BACK TO WORK.
JOSEP AND THE AMAZIN TECHNI-COLOR SADDLE
FREAK OUT
!
SEDAN CHAIR
A... A REFUND?
R BITS ACK?
WELL, ONLY HALF OF IT. I DID ACTUALLY STAY FOR A FEW DAYS... BUT, WELL, THIS REALLY ISN'T MY IDEA OF RELAXATION. I'D RATHER GO HOME AND WORK ON...
RARITY, I'M SO RRY... WE, WELL, LREADY SPENT THE BITS YOU PAID US.
YOU COULD, LIKE, UM, HAVE SOME OF WHEAT'S CARROT-CARROB-AND-BEAN CRUNCHY CLUSTERS?
YOU ALREADY SPENT IT? CARROTCAROBWHAT? WHAT ARE YOU TALKING ABOUT?
THEY'RE CRUNCHY BECAUSE SHE USES DRIED BEANS. FIBER!
OH, RARITY. I'M SO SORRY. THIS ISN'T YOUR PROBLEM. YOU SEE, WE'RE ABOUT TO LOSE THE LAND THE FARM IS ON! WE MADE A TERRIBLE DEAL WITH SOME PONIES NAMED "FLIM" AND "FLAM"... IF WE DON'T PAY THEM BY THE END OF THE MONTH, THEY GET THE FARM AND THEY'RE SELLING IT TO BARNYARD BARGAINS SO FILTHY RICH CAN BUILD A NEW MEGASTORE.

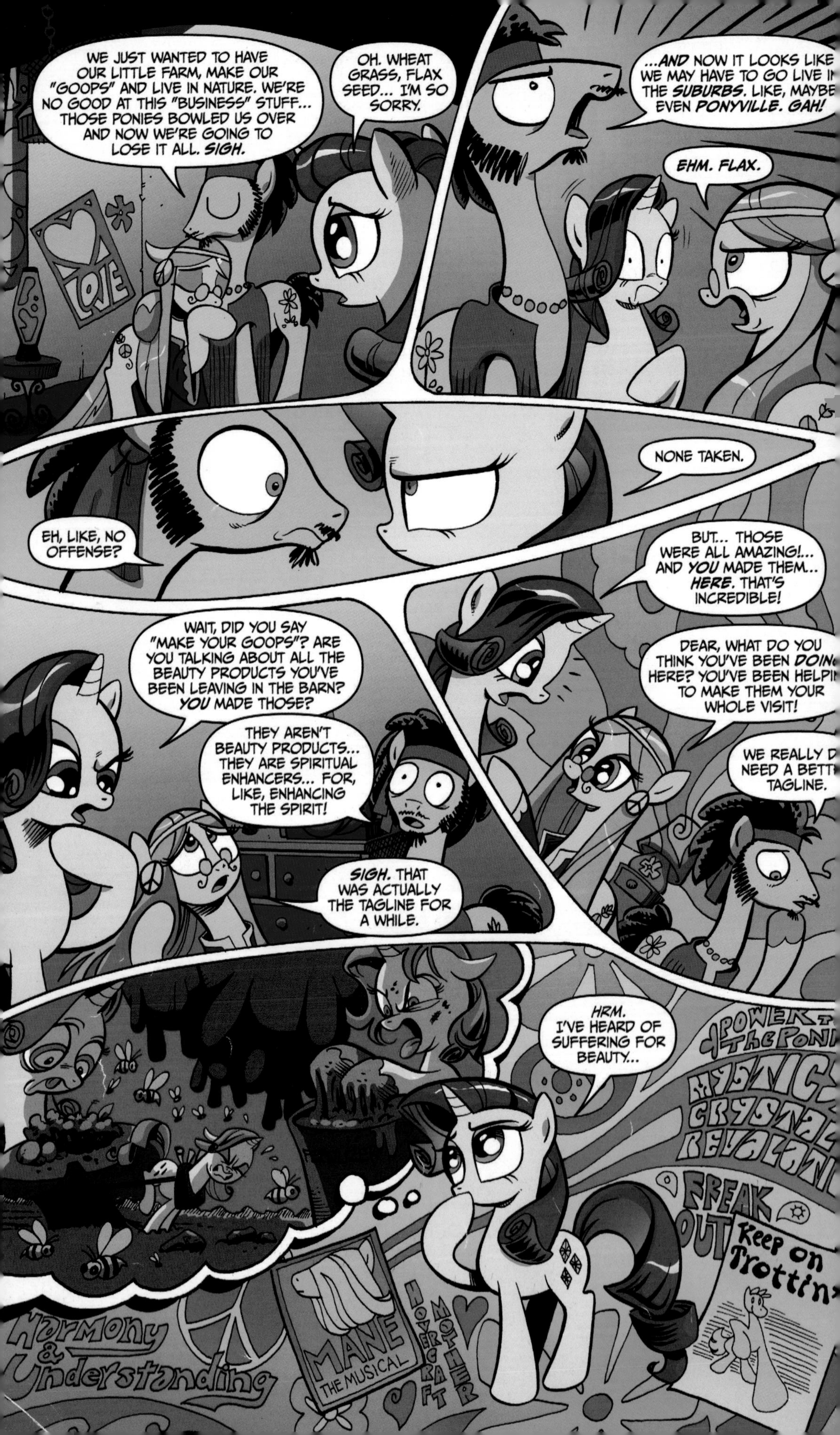
WE JUST WANTED TO HAVE OUR LITTLE FARM, MAKE OUR "GOOPS" AND LIVE IN NATURE. WE'RE NO GOOD AT THIS "BUSINESS" STUFF... THOSE PONIES BOWLED US OVER AND NOW WE'RE GOING TO LOSE IT ALL. SIGH.
OH. WHEAT GRASS, FLAX SEED... I'M SO SORRY.
LOVE
...AND NOW IT LOOKS LIKE WE MAY HAVE TO GO LIVE IN THE SUBURBS. LIKE, MAYBE EVEN PONYVILLE. GAH!
EHM. FLAX.
EH, LIKE, NO OFFENSE?
NONE TAKEN.
WAIT, DID YOU SAY "MAKE YOUR GOOPS"? ARE YOU TALKING ABOUT ALL THE BEAUTY PRODUCTS YOU'VE BEEN LEAVING IN THE BARN? YOU MADE THOSE?
THEY AREN'T BEAUTY PRODUCTS... THEY ARE SPIRITUAL ENHANCERS... FOR, LIKE, ENHANCING THE SPIRIT!
SIGH. THAT WAS ACTUALLY THE TAGLINE FOR A WHILE.
BUT... THOSE WERE ALL AMAZING!... AND YOU MADE THEM... HERE. THAT'S INCREDIBLE!
DEAR, WHAT DO YOU THINK YOU'VE BEEN DOIN HERE? YOU'VE BEEN HELPIN TO MAKE THEM YOUR WHOLE VISIT!
WE REALLY D NEED A BETT TAGLINE.
HRM. I'VE HEARD OF SUFFERING FOR BEAUTY...
FREAK OUT
Keep on Trottin'
Harmony & Understanding
MANE THE MUSICAL
HOVERCRAFT MOTHER

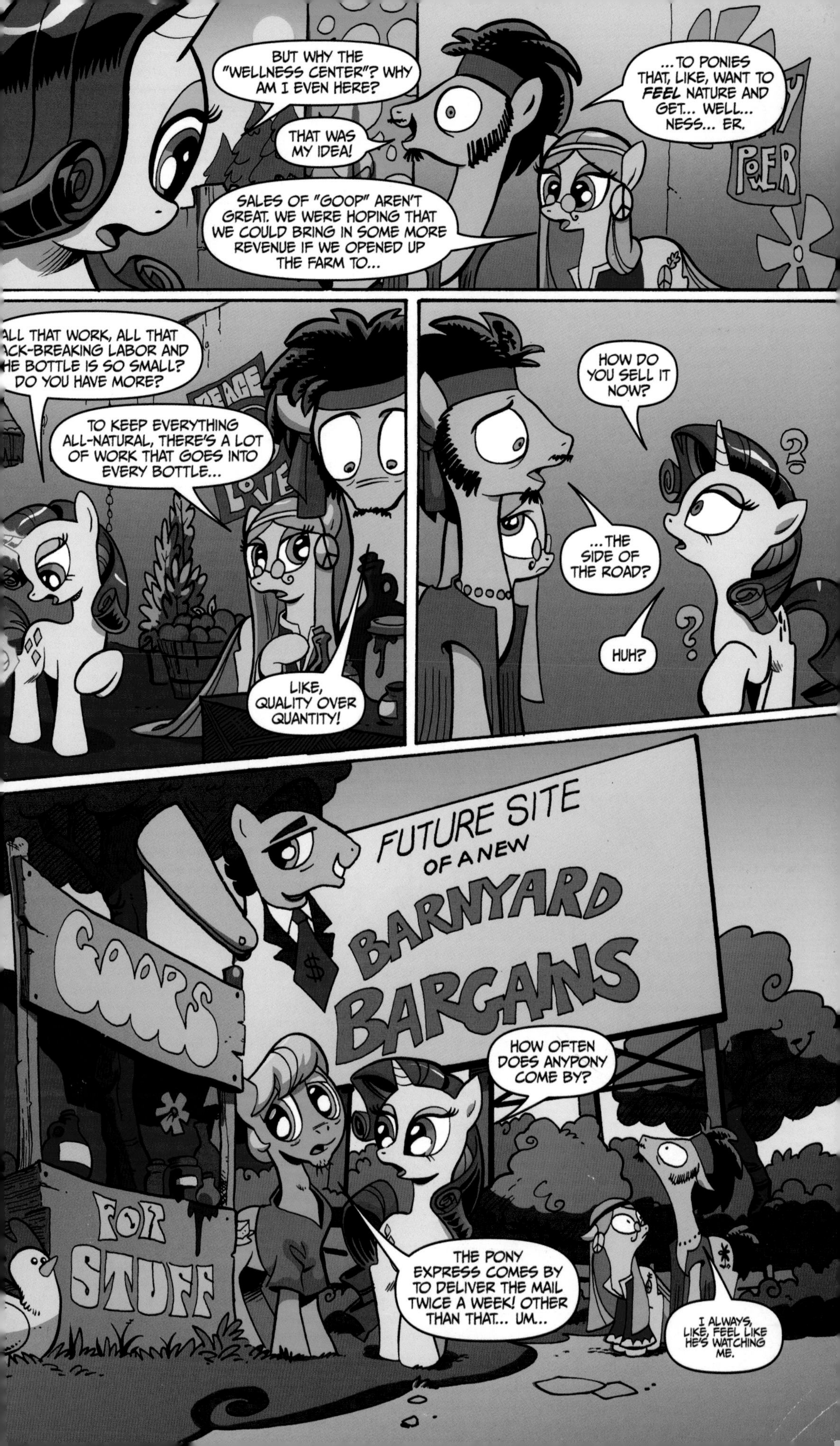
BUT WHY THE "WELLNESS CENTER"? WHY AM I EVEN HERE?
THAT WAS MY IDEA!
SALES OF "GOOP" AREN'T GREAT. WE WERE HOPING THAT WE COULD BRING IN SOME MORE REVENUE IF WE OPENED UP THE FARM TO...
...TO PONIES THAT, LIKE, WANT TO FEEL NATURE AND GET... WELL... NESS... ER.
POWER
ALL THAT WORK, ALL THAT ACK-BREAKING LABOR AND HE BOTTLE IS SO SMALL? DO YOU HAVE MORE?
TO KEEP EVERYTHING ALL-NATURAL, THERE'S A LOT OF WORK THAT GOES INTO EVERY BOTTLE...
LOVE
LIKE, QUALITY OVER QUANTITY!
HOW DO YOU SELL IT NOW?
...THE SIDE OF THE ROAD?
HUH?
FUTURE SITE OF A NEW BARNYARD BARGAINS
GOOPS
FOR STUFF
HOW OFTEN DOES ANYPONY COME BY?
THE PONY EXPRESS COMES BY TO DELIVER THE MAIL TWICE A WEEK! OTHER THAN THAT... UM...
I ALWAYS, LIKE, FEEL LIKE HE'S WATCHING ME.

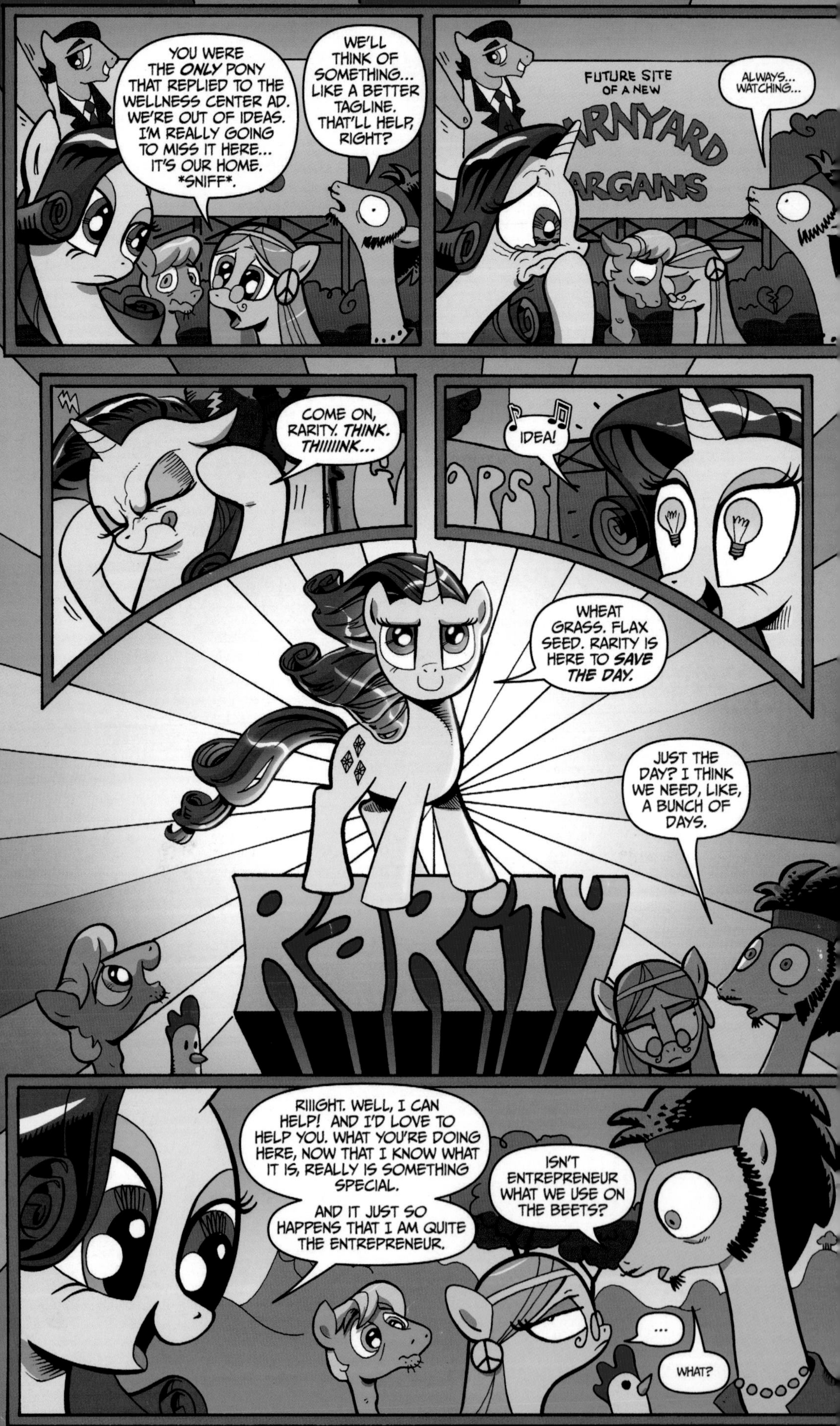

YOU WERE THE ONLY PONY THAT REPLIED TO THE WELLNESS CENTER AD. WE'RE OUT OF IDEAS. I'M REALLY GOING TO MISS IT HERE... IT'S OUR HOME. *SNIFF*.
WE'LL THINK OF SOMETHING... LIKE A BETTER TAGLINE. THAT'LL HELP, RIGHT?
FUTURE SITE OF A NEW
RNYARD
ARGAINS
ALWAYS... WATCHING...
COME ON, RARITY. THINK. THIIIIINK...
IDEA!
WHEAT GRASS. FLAX SEED. RARITY IS HERE TO SAVE THE DAY.
JUST THE DAY? I THINK WE NEED, LIKE, A BUNCH OF DAYS.
RARITY
RIIIGHT. WELL, I CAN HELP! AND I'D LOVE TO HELP YOU. WHAT YOU'RE DOING HERE, NOW THAT I KNOW WHAT IT IS, REALLY IS SOMETHING SPECIAL.
AND IT JUST SO HAPPENS THAT I AM QUITE THE ENTREPRENEUR.
ISN'T ENTREPRENEUR WHAT WE USE ON THE BEETS?
...
WHAT?

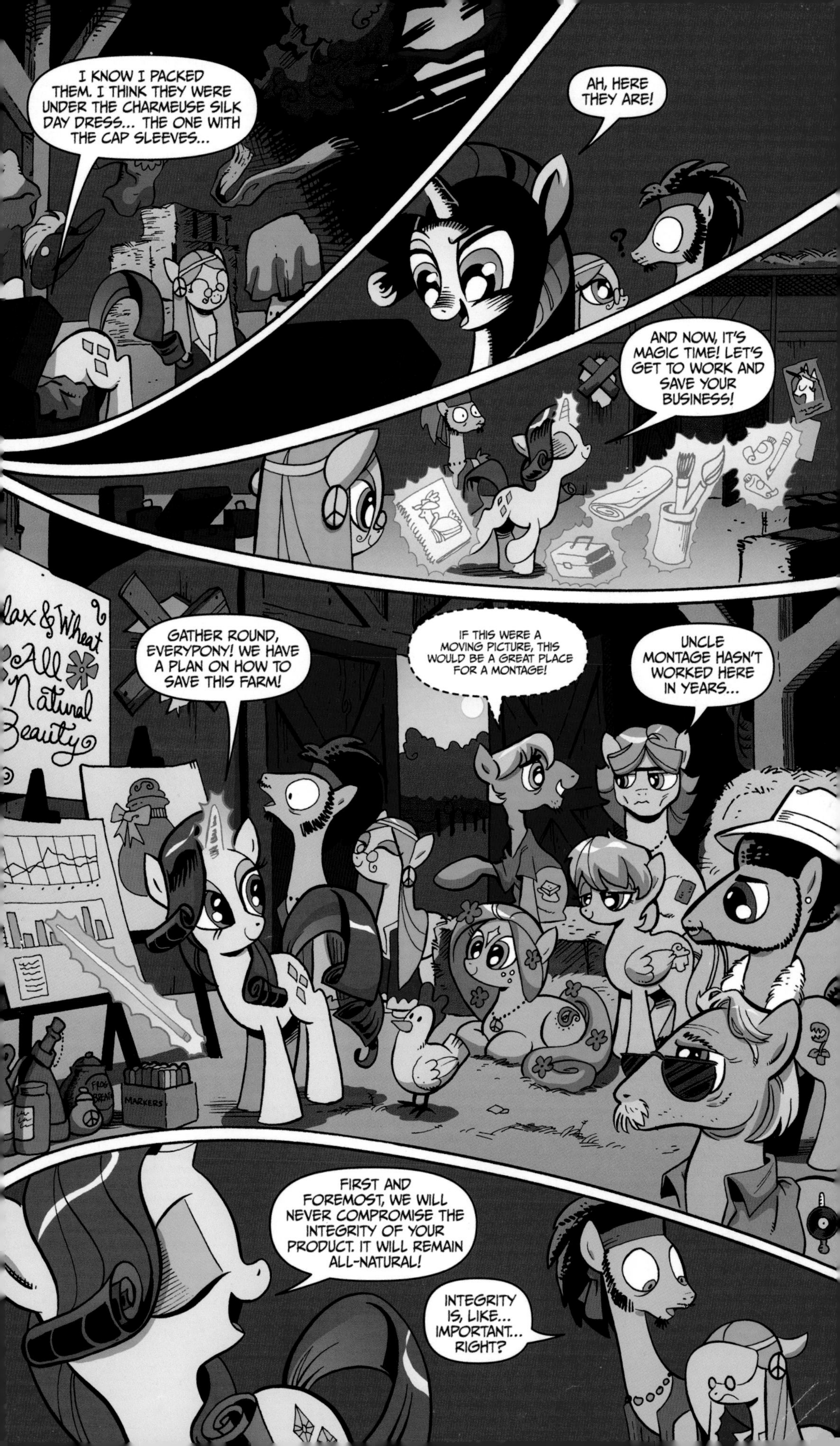
I KNOW I PACKED THEM. I THINK THEY WERE UNDER THE CHARMEUSE SILK DAY DRESS... THE ONE WITH THE CAP SLEEVES...
AH, HERE THEY ARE!
?
AND NOW, IT'S MAGIC TIME! LET'S GET TO WORK AND SAVE YOUR BUSINESS!
Flax & Wheat All Natural Beauty
GATHER ROUND, EVERYPONY! WE HAVE A PLAN ON HOW TO SAVE THIS FARM!
IF THIS WERE A MOVING PICTURE, THIS WOULD BE A GREAT PLACE FOR A MONTAGE!
UNCLE MONTAGE HASN'T WORKED HERE IN YEARS...
MARKERS
FROG
FIRST AND FOREMOST, WE WILL NEVER COMPROMISE THE INTEGRITY OF YOUR PRODUCT. IT WILL REMAIN ALL-NATURAL!
INTEGRITY IS, LIKE... IMPORTANT... RIGHT?

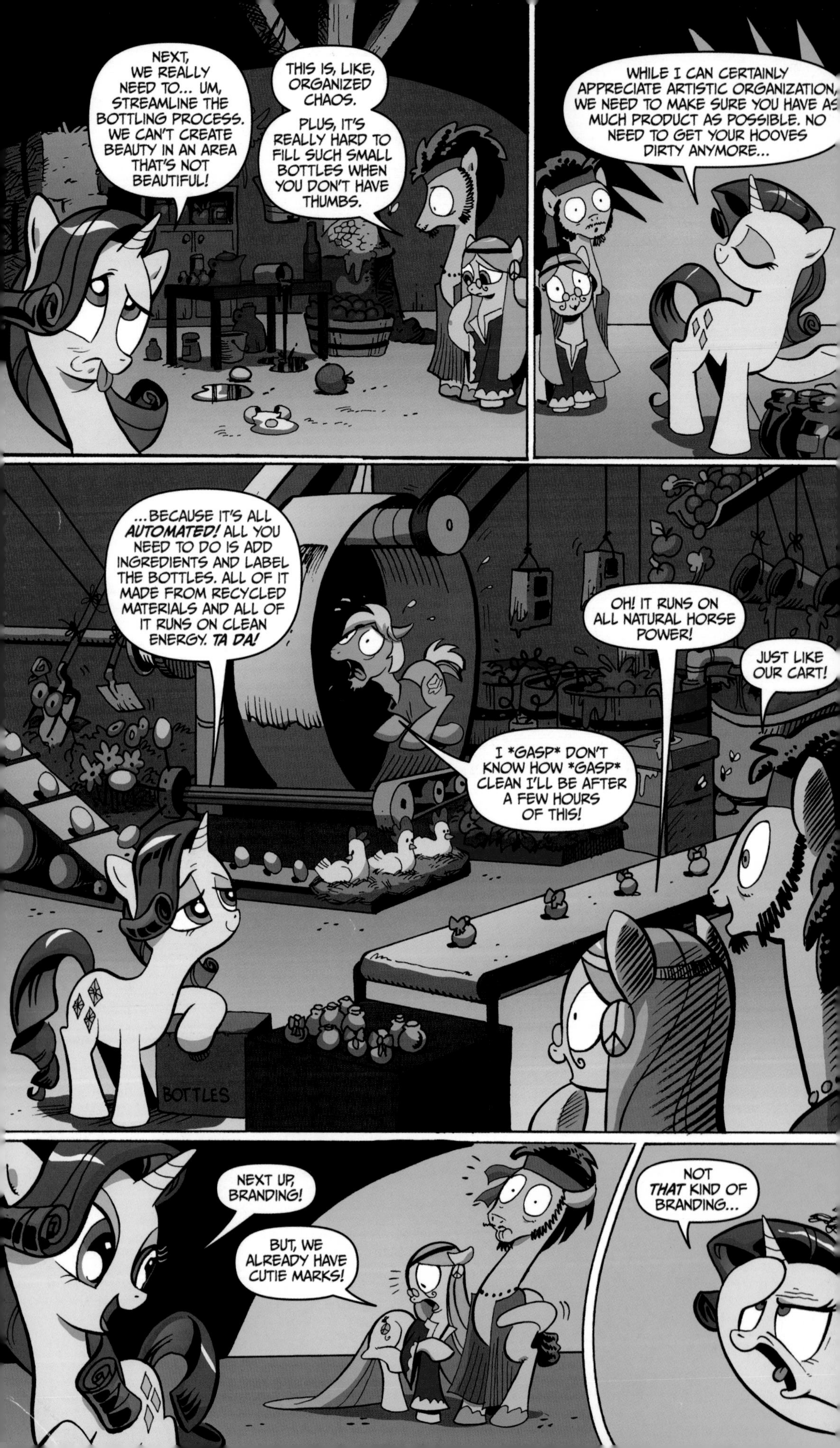
NEXT, WE REALLY NEED TO... UM, STREAMLINE THE BOTTLING PROCESS. WE CAN'T CREATE BEAUTY IN AN AREA THAT'S NOT BEAUTIFUL!
THIS IS, LIKE, ORGANIZED CHAOS.
PLUS, IT'S REALLY HARD TO FILL SUCH SMALL BOTTLES WHEN YOU DON'T HAVE THUMBS.
WHILE I CAN CERTAINLY APPRECIATE ARTISTIC ORGANIZATION, WE NEED TO MAKE SURE YOU HAVE AS MUCH PRODUCT AS POSSIBLE. NO NEED TO GET YOUR HOOVES DIRTY ANYMORE...
...BECAUSE IT'S ALL AUTOMATED! ALL YOU NEED TO DO IS ADD INGREDIENTS AND LABEL THE BOTTLES. ALL OF IT MADE FROM RECYCLED MATERIALS AND ALL OF IT RUNS ON CLEAN ENERGY. TA DA!
I *GASP* DON'T KNOW HOW *GASP* CLEAN I'LL BE AFTER A FEW HOURS OF THIS!
OH! IT RUNS ON ALL NATURAL HORSE POWER!
JUST LIKE OUR CART!
BOTTLES
NEXT UP, BRANDING!
BUT, WE ALREADY HAVE CUTIE MARKS!
NOT THAT KIND OF BRANDING...

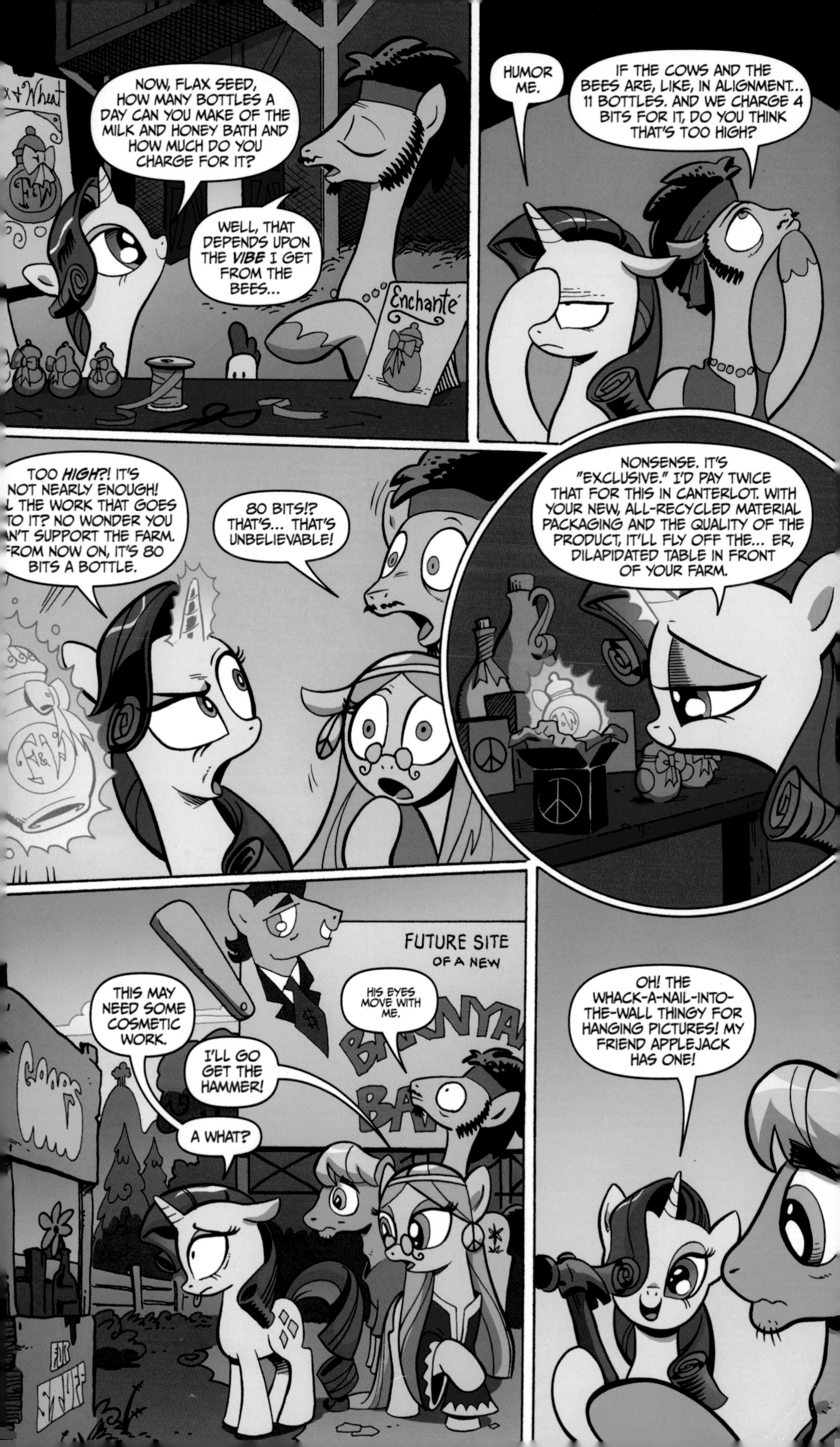
NOW, FLAX SEED, HOW MANY BOTTLES A DAY CAN YOU MAKE OF THE MILK AND HONEY BATH AND HOW MUCH DO YOU CHARGE FOR IT?
WELL, THAT DEPENDS UPON THE VIBE I GET FROM THE BEES...
Enchanté
HUMOR ME.
IF THE COWS AND THE BEES ARE, LIKE, IN ALIGNMENT... 11 BOTTLES. AND WE CHARGE 4 BITS FOR IT, DO YOU THINK THAT'S TOO HIGH?
TOO HIGH?! IT'S NOT NEARLY ENOUGH! ALL THE WORK THAT GOES INTO IT? NO WONDER YOU CAN'T SUPPORT THE FARM. FROM NOW ON, IT'S 80 BITS A BOTTLE.
80 BITS!? THAT'S... THAT'S UNBELIEVABLE!
NONSENSE. IT'S "EXCLUSIVE." I'D PAY TWICE THAT FOR THIS IN CANTERLOT. WITH YOUR NEW, ALL-RECYCLED MATERIAL PACKAGING AND THE QUALITY OF THE PRODUCT, IT'LL FLY OFF THE... ER, DILAPIDATED TABLE IN FRONT OF YOUR FARM.
FUTURE SITE OF A NEW
THIS MAY NEED SOME COSMETIC WORK.
HIS EYES MOVE WITH ME.
I'LL GO GET THE HAMMER!
A WHAT?
OH! THE WHACK-A-NAIL-INTO-THE-WALL THINGY FOR HANGING PICTURES! MY FRIEND APPLEJACK HAS ONE!

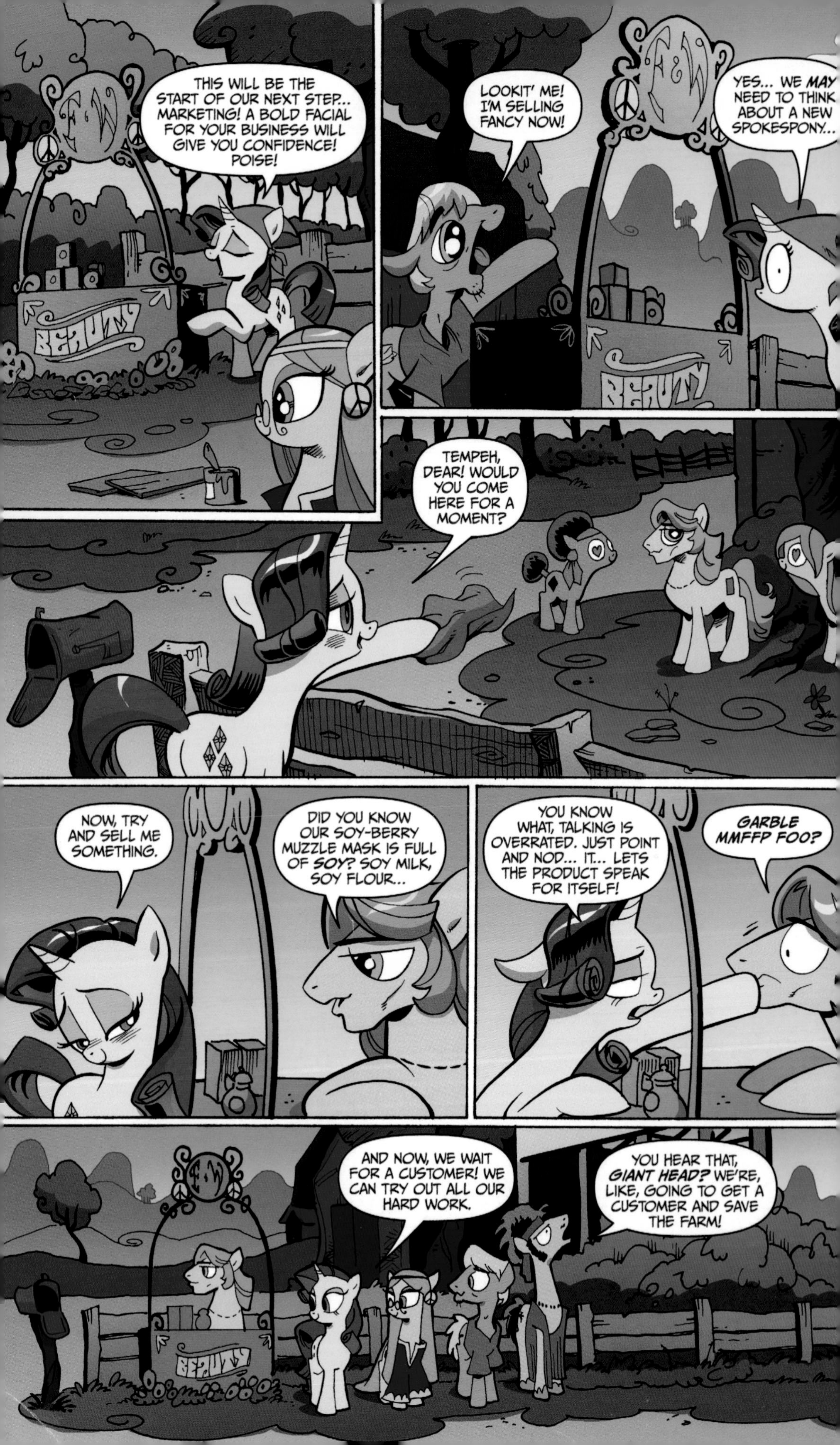

THIS WILL BE THE START OF OUR NEXT STEP... MARKETING! A BOLD FACIAL FOR YOUR BUSINESS WILL GIVE YOU CONFIDENCE! POISE!
BEAUTY
LOOKIT' ME! I'M SELLING FANCY NOW!
YES... WE *MAY* NEED TO THINK ABOUT A NEW SPOKESPONY...
BEAUTY
TEMPEH, DEAR! WOULD YOU COME HERE FOR A MOMENT?
NOW, TRY AND SELL ME SOMETHING.
DID YOU KNOW OUR SOY-BERRY MUZZLE MASK IS FULL OF *SOY?* SOY MILK, SOY FLOUR...
YOU KNOW WHAT, TALKING IS OVERRATED. JUST POINT AND NOD... IT... LETS THE PRODUCT SPEAK FOR ITSELF!
GARBLE MMFFP FOO?
AND NOW, WE WAIT FOR A CUSTOMER! WE CAN TRY OUT ALL OUR HARD WORK.
YOU HEAR THAT, *GIANT HEAD?* WE'RE, LIKE, GOING TO GET A CUSTOMER AND SAVE THE FARM!
BEAUTY

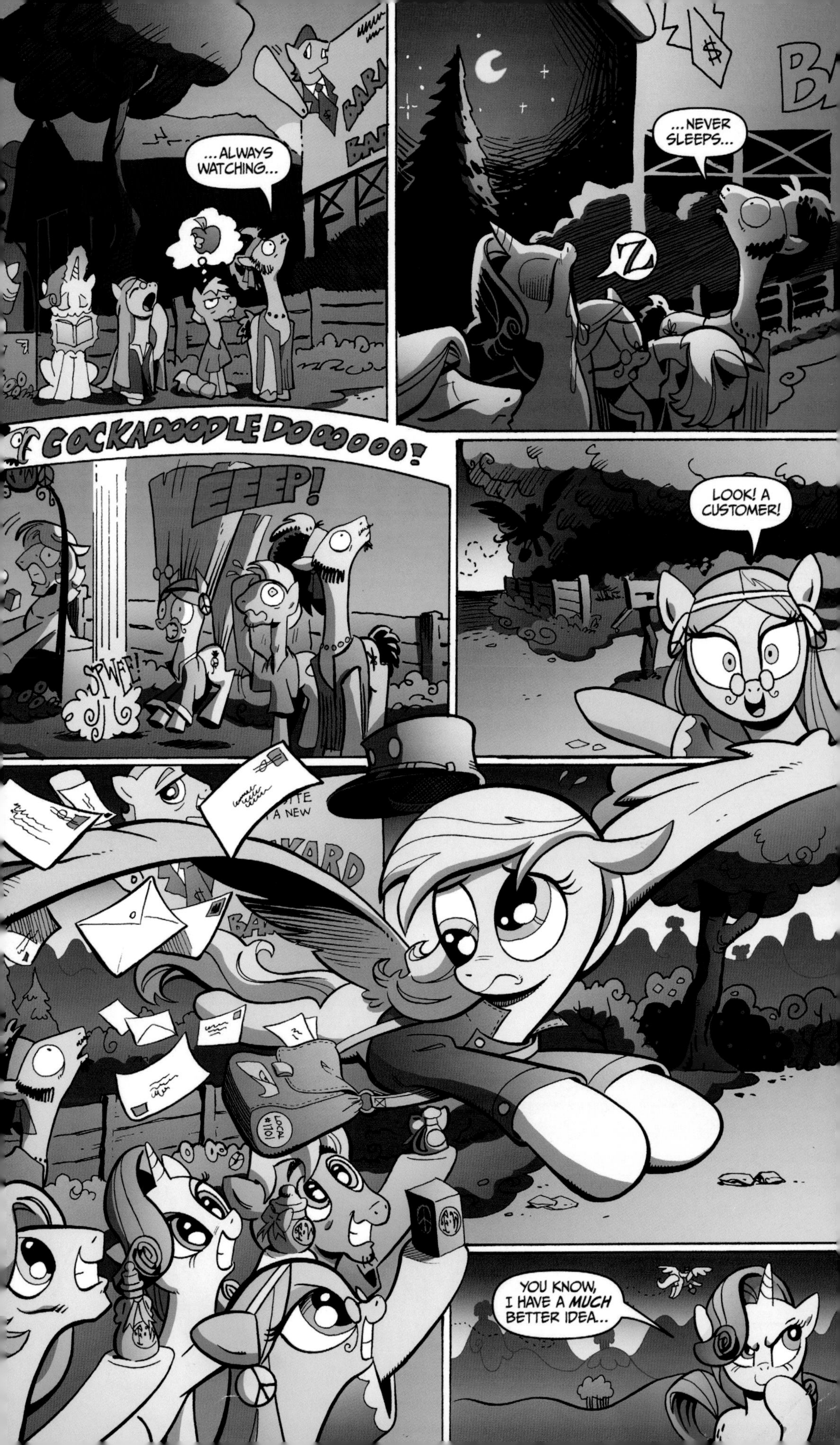
...ALWAYS WATCHING...
...NEVER SLEEPS...
Z
COCKADOODLE DOOOOOOO!
EEEP!
SPWEE!
LOOK! A CUSTOMER!
LOCAL #110!
YOU KNOW, I HAVE A *MUCH* BETTER IDEA...

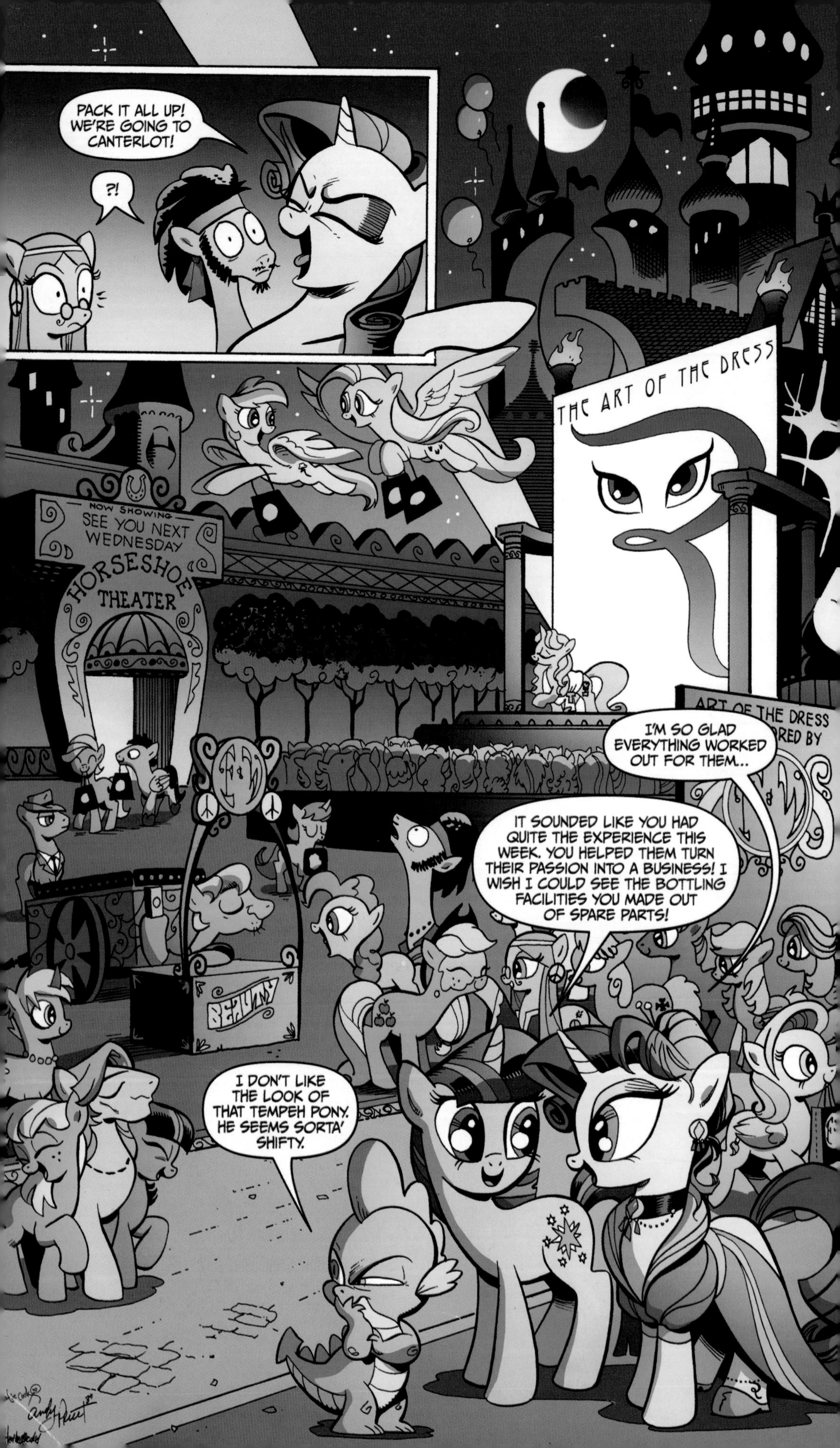
PACK IT ALL UP! WE'RE GOING TO CANTERLOT!
?!
THE ART OF THE DRESS
NOW SHOWING
SEE YOU NEXT WEDNESDAY
HORSESHOE THEATER
ART OF THE DRESS
I'M SO GLAD EVERYTHING WORKED OUT FOR THEM...
IT SOUNDED LIKE YOU HAD QUITE THE EXPERIENCE THIS WEEK. YOU HELPED THEM TURN THEIR PASSION INTO A BUSINESS! I WISH I COULD SEE THE BOTTLING FACILITIES YOU MADE OUT OF SPARE PARTS!
I DON'T LIKE THE LOOK OF THAT TEMPEH PONY. HE SEEMS SORTA' SHIFTY.

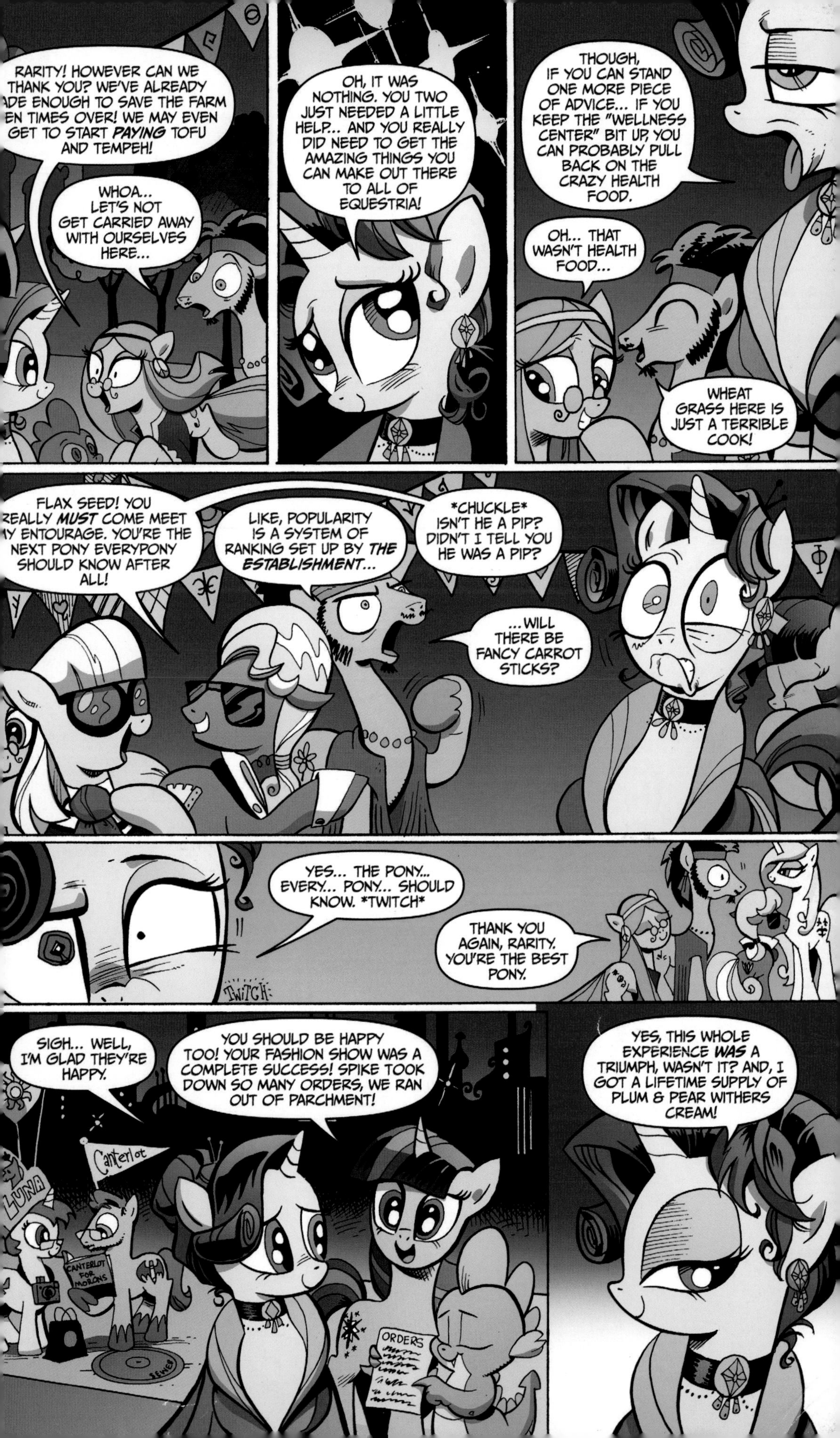
RARITY! HOWEVER CAN WE THANK YOU? WE'VE ALREADY ADE ENOUGH TO SAVE THE FARM EN TIMES OVER! WE MAY EVEN GET TO START **PAYING** TOFU AND TEMPEH!
WHOA... LET'S NOT GET CARRIED AWAY WITH OURSELVES HERE...
OH, IT WAS NOTHING. YOU TWO JUST NEEDED A LITTLE HELP... AND YOU REALLY DID NEED TO GET THE AMAZING THINGS YOU CAN MAKE OUT THERE TO ALL OF EQUESTRIA!
THOUGH, IF YOU CAN STAND ONE MORE PIECE OF ADVICE... IF YOU KEEP THE "WELLNESS CENTER" BIT UP, YOU CAN PROBABLY PULL BACK ON THE CRAZY HEALTH FOOD.
OH... THAT WASN'T HEALTH FOOD...
WHEAT GRASS HERE IS JUST A TERRIBLE COOK!
FLAX SEED! YOU EALLY **MUST** COME MEET Y ENTOURAGE. YOU'RE THE NEXT PONY EVERYPONY SHOULD KNOW AFTER ALL!
LIKE, POPULARITY IS A SYSTEM OF RANKING SET UP BY ***THE ESTABLISHMENT***...
CHUCKLE ISN'T HE A PIP? DIDN'T I TELL YOU HE WAS A PIP?
...WILL THERE BE FANCY CARROT STICKS?
YES... THE PONY... EVERY... PONY... SHOULD KNOW. *TWITCH*
TWITCH
THANK YOU AGAIN, RARITY. YOU'RE THE BEST PONY.
SIGH... WELL, I'M GLAD THEY'RE HAPPY.
YOU SHOULD BE HAPPY TOO! YOUR FASHION SHOW WAS A COMPLETE SUCCESS! SPIKE TOOK DOWN SO MANY ORDERS, WE RAN OUT OF PARCHMENT!
Canterlot
LUNA
CANTERLOT FOR MORONS
ORDERS
YES, THIS WHOLE EXPERIENCE **WAS** A TRIUMPH, WASN'T IT? AND, I GOT A LIFETIME SUPPLY OF PLUM & PEAR WITHERS CREAM!

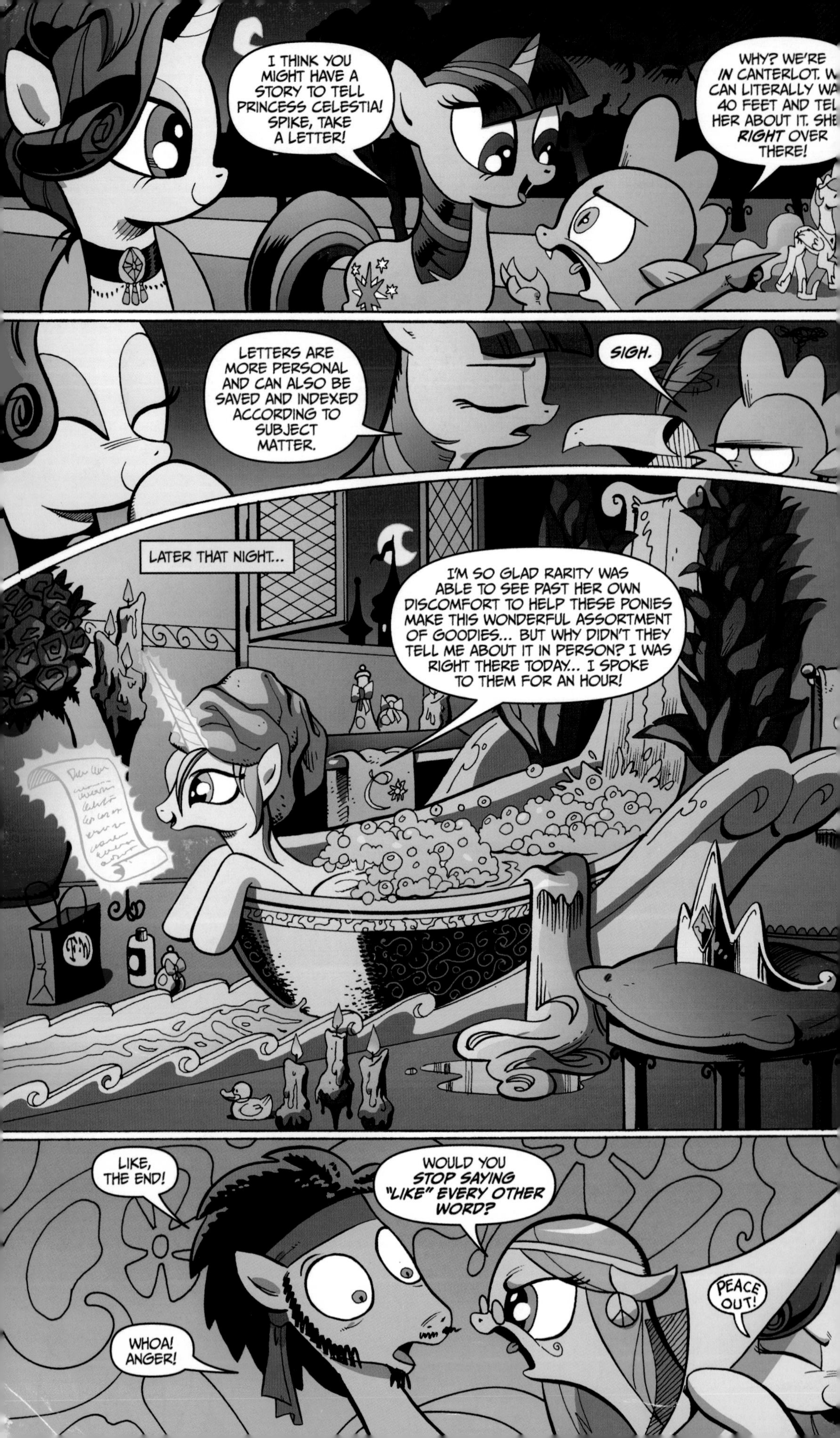
I THINK YOU MIGHT HAVE A STORY TO TELL PRINCESS CELESTIA! SPIKE, TAKE A LETTER!
WHY? WE'RE *IN* CANTERLOT. W CAN LITERALLY WA 40 FEET AND TEL HER ABOUT IT. SHE *RIGHT* OVER THERE!
LETTERS ARE MORE PERSONAL AND CAN ALSO BE SAVED AND INDEXED ACCORDING TO SUBJECT MATTER.
SIGH.
LATER THAT NIGHT...
I'M SO GLAD RARITY WAS ABLE TO SEE PAST HER OWN DISCOMFORT TO HELP THESE PONIES MAKE THIS WONDERFUL ASSORTMENT OF GOODIES... BUT WHY DIDN'T THEY TELL ME ABOUT IT IN PERSON? I WAS RIGHT THERE TODAY... I SPOKE TO THEM FOR AN HOUR!
LIKE, THE END!
WOULD YOU *STOP SAYING "LIKE" EVERY OTHER WORD?*
PEACE OUT!
WHOA! ANGER!